The hardcase dipped his free hand into a pocket and brought out a squat heavy-calibred Derringer Pocket Pistol. Before he could bring his weapon into line, the man saw the newcomer look, then swing the right arm in his direction. Something leathery-feeling curled around the man's wrist, gripping it in a sudden vice-like hold that crushed the bones and snapped them like rotten twigs. A scream burst from the man's lips, and the Derringer clattered unfired to the ground.

*It was tough on the hardcase that Martha Jane Canary had appeared on the scene. The girl everyone knew as Calamity Jane was no ordinary female.*

# J T EDSON

## THE
## BULL WHIP BREED

CORGI BOOKS
A DIVISION OF TRANSWORLD PUBLISHERS

THE BULL WHIP BREED

A CORGI BOOK 552 08011 X

Originally published in Great Britain
by Brown Watson Limited

PRINTING HISTORY
Corgi Edition published 1968

Copyright © 1968 by Transworld Publishers Ltd.

This book is set in 9-10 pt. Plantin

Corgi Books are published by Transworld Publishers Ltd.,
Bashley Road, London, N.W.10.
Made and printed in Great Britain by
Hunt Barnard & Co. Ltd., Aylesbury, Bucks.

# CHAPTER ONE

## *Lieutenant St Andre Meets An Unusual Lady*

PHILIPPE St. Andre was said to be the youngest and most handsome man ever to reach the rank of lieutenant on the New Orleans police force. Only he did not seem likely to remain the most handsome for much longer. The four bulky, burly men who came from the shadows of the dark, narrow street intended to alter the shape of his face, or St. Andre missed his guess. While a bright moon shone in the sky, very little of its light filtered down into the area between the houses; which might be ideal for lovers, or even people who merely wished to act in the manner of lovers, but was surely hell for a handsome young detective lieutenant faced with the possibility of a savage beating. He could neither see their faces nor enough of their clothing to be able to recognise them at a later date—should they leave him alive to do so.

"Are you St. Andre?" asked the biggest man in a muffled, disguised voice.

"I am."

"Then you get after Vivian Vanderlyne and don't go poking your nose into things that don't concern you."

Instantly St. Andre clenched his fists and prepared to fight for his life.

While St. Andre had been born into one of the oldest, richest and proudest New Orleans families, and dressed, now he was a member of the newly-formed detective bureau of the police department, to the height of fashion, he was also a trained and very smart peace officer who knew his way around.

Following a lead in his current case brought him to the dark side-street and he knew the four hard-cases had not stopped him merely to pass the time of day. Ever since starting his investigation into the murder of Vance Cornwall, a prominently rising young lawyer, St. Andre's lawman instincts told him that the affair cut much deeper than a lovers' quarrel which went too far. Cornwall had been a married man, with a very rich, if much older, woman for his wife; an ill-tempered shrew, if all rumours be true, so Cornwall sought solace by taking an *amie*. Most of the evidence pointed to Cornwall's *amie* having done the killing, but the blonde, beautiful and talented young actress, Vivian Vanderlyne, appeared to have done the opposite, disappeared, for no trace of her could be found.*

The murder appeared to be an open-and-shut case, a trifle sordid maybe, but ordinary. Yet St. Andre felt that certain facts did not fit into the picture of a lovers' quarrel ending in violent death. Why had the murdered man's rooms been thoroughly searched? From whence came the faint smell of expensive perfume which mingled and clashed with a slightly cheaper brand used by Vivian Vanderlyne?

Being a conscientious lawman, St. Andre tried to find the answers to his questions. While following up the most obvious suspect, he also went to visit the dead man's wife and brother, asking questions and finding both to have perfect alibis for the time of the killing. So St. Andre looked elsewhere and a tip from an informer brought him to the side road and the waiting quartet. Somebody clearly did not want too close an investigation into the young lawyer's private life. It would seem that St. Andre's lawman instincts were correct—only he did not appear to be likely to stay alive long enough to solve the mystery.

"And if I don't?" he asked, measuring his distances.

The first blow hissed over his head as he ducked. Coming up inside the striker's guard, St. Andre threw his well-manicured, but rock-hard fist under a bristle-covered, bandana-masked jaw with enough power to send the first attacker staggering backwards. In almost the same movement, as the man he hit went away spluttering curses, St. Andre pivoted around and delivered a stamping kick to the pit of the second man's belly. Continuing his turn with the fluid grace of a ballet dancer, St. Andre shifted his weight to his rear foot, drew his raised right leg up and in front of the left and lifted his body slightly on the ball of the left foot. The crossing of the right leg gave it greater distance to move and provide extra momentum and kicking power. How effective the *chasse croise*, or front lateral kick of *savate*, proved showed in the way the second man went down as St. Andre lashed up and sideways with his right foot, leaning his body away from the recipient and delivering a slashing, stabbing kick at the jaw.

After which the ball ended and the piper requested payment. The third man's fist came driving into St. Andre's cheek as the detective returned to his fighting stance and before he could take any further action. Caught by the blow, St. Andre shot across the

*For further details of the Vanderlyne case read THE MAN FROM TEXAS by J. T. Edson.

street and collided with the left side wall. Before he could recover, the fourth man sank a fist into his stomach and jack-knifed him over. Bringing up his left knee, the man smashed it into St. Andre's face, jerking the detective erect again with blood gushing from his nostrils.

"Fix him!" roared a voice.

Through the roaring pain-mists which engulfed him, St. Andre saw the four men coming at him and his fighting instincts reacted to the situation faster than could his spinning brain. Like a flash St. Andre brought up his right foot in a kick which sent the toe to catch the closest of the quartet *real* low and in a manner which would have caused the detective's instant disqualification if used in a sporting contest at Duval's *Savate* Academy. However St. Andre was not indulging in a sporting contest, but fighting for his life. So he drove his toe into his nearest attacker's stomach and sent the man stumbling from the fray in moaning, doubled-over agony.

Fists thudded into St. Andre's face and body, savage blows that drove pain through him. While he hit and kicked back— *savate* permitted the use of the hands as well as the feet—St. Andre knew it to be merely a matter of time before the remaining trio reduced him to a bloody, battered, broken wreck. Fighting on through the beating, St. Andre tried to so mark his attackers that identifying them would be comparatively easy. Not that he was likely to be in any condition mentally or physically to do any identifying unless he received help quickly.

It may be that at that moment St. Andre became the first man to think, "There is never a policeman around when you need one," for mister, he needed not one but a good dozen big, brawny policemen's aid just about as badly as anybody in the whole United States at that moment—or five minutes earlier if it came to a point.

A passer-by walked along the street which intersected the one down which the trio of hard-cases practiced playing in the percussion section of an orchestra, using St. Andre's body instead of a drum. While most people in a city like New Orleans might have glanced at the disturbance, they knew sufficient about the facts of life to show their interest in the welfare of others by walking away hurriedly. Not so the slim, somewhat boyish shape, for it came to a halt, then started heading along the street towards the struggling group of men.

Turning from St. Andre, one of the attacking trio let out a bellow of rage calculated to scare off even the most nosey citizen.

"Get the hell out of here!" he bellowed. "Shift it, or you'll get some of the same."

At that moment one of the men was landing a kick into St. Andre's ribs, while the second gripped the detective's hair, held his head back and smashed the other hand into a bloody face; St. Andre being on his knees and, although just about conscious, too far gone to defend himself. It was a sight, taken with the third hard-case's warning, liable to scare off anybody with an interest in their own well-being, no matter how much they might wish to help the sufferer.

Only neither the warning nor the sight appeared to frighten and drive off the slim intruder. Taking in the boyish build of the new-comer, the tough who gave the warning started forward, intending to carry out his threat. Skidding to a halt, the newcomer shot a right hand under the left side of an open jacket and brought something, most likely a weapon thought the burly tough out from beneath the coat's flap. Not a gun or a knife, the tough saw to his relief, but what at first glance appeared to be a two foot long police baton. Matched against a burly, six foot tall, one hundred and ninety pound rough-neck, that boyish shape, at the most five foot seven in height and not heavily built with it, did not appear to be showing good sense in relying on such a puny weapon.

Which only went to show how wrong appearances sometimes are.

Even before the tough came within arm's length, in fact while he was still several feet away, the newcomer's arm raised and swung down again. For a moment the tough thought that the newcomer had panicked and tried to throw the club at him. It proved to be his last coherent thought for some time. Something hissed through the air towards the tough and cracked like a pistol shot. Instantly the burly man's face felt as if it had burst into flames. Bright lights seemed to be exploding before the tough's eyes and he reeled backwards, hands clawing at the blood which oozed from a mysterious gash that had suddenly appeared across his face, running from his right temple down to the lobe of his left ear.

Hearing their pard's screech of agony, the other two men swung away from St. Andre and prepared to take retaliatory measures against the brash intruder who dared come between them and their prey. Being experts in their particular line of work, if complete and utter failures at any task requiring brains or finesse, the hard-cases liked to give good service when sent on a mission. So they figured working over an inquisitive interloper would give them just a little more of the practice all men know makes perfect.

Unfortunately for the men, that slim newcomer did not intend to take a brutal beating in the interests of helping them perfect their technique. Again and again the intruder's right arm swung up and down, each time being followed by a hissing crack and a yell or howl of pain from one of the trio of attackers. All the time a flow of hide-blistering invective, in a voice raised by either fear or excitement to what sounded almost like a woman's tones, flowed from the intruder.

Nor did St. Andre's saviour remain content to stand back and use whatever weapon caused such consternation among the detective's attackers, but moved forward step by step in an attempt to drive the hard-cases away. St. Andre tried to force himself to his feet so as to lend his rescuer a helping hand. However the pain and exhaustion spawned by his beating prevented him from rising, nor could his spinning senses give the order to draw out his police whistle and summon aid. While the newcomer seemed to be handling things quite satisfactorily, St. Andre wanted to capture his attackers if possible. A good peace officer always liked to know who sent men to attack and beat him up; and not entirely for personal reasons.

"Agh!" howled the biggest man, following one of the cracking noises. "Do something, Max!"

His words appeared to be directed at the man St. Andre put out of the fight with a low kick. Holding his injured region with one hand, the man crawled painfully to his feet. However, on hearing his friend's shout, the man dipped his free hand into a pocket and brought out a squat, heavy calibred Derringer Pocket Pistol. Before he could bring his weapon into line, the man saw the newcomer look, then swing the right arm in his direction. Something leathery-feeling curled around the man's wrist, gripping it in a sudden, frightening, vice-like hold that crushed the bones and snapped them like rotten twigs. A scream burst from the man's lips as a fresh pain almost made him forget his previous injury, and the Derringer clattered unfired to the ground.

"Let's get out of here!" one of the quartet yelled.

Panic had always been infectious and so it proved in this case. Shaken by the inexplicable pain caused by whatever kind of weapon the intruder held, knowing that at any moment St. Andre might recover enough to start blowing his whistle to summon help, and having a fair idea of their fate if captured by the police after attacking and brutally beating a popular member of the legion of the blue, the four hard-cases decided enough to be sufficient for the day. Having reached that conclusion, they decided to chance their employer's wrath at failing to do a *real* good job on St. Andre. So they turned and took to their heels, racing away down the street, leaving a sick and sorry police lieutenant and a slim boyish-looking shape in possession of the field.

After the sound of the quartet's footsteps died away, the intruder turned and walked towards St. Andre. Coiling the lash of the long bull-whip handled with such deadly precision, the newcomer thrust it back under the jacket and bent to help a groaning St. Andre to rise.

At first the detective thought of asking his rescuer to take out his whistle and blow on it to summon aid. Then he realised that there would be little chance of catching the four men. If he knew their kind, and he reckoned he did, they would have a good escape route planned and be away before the police managed to surround the area.

Taking St. Andre by the arm, the newcomer started to lift as he struggled to get to his feet. Weakly he reached towards the other, wanting to get support for a pair of legs which hardly seemed capable of supporting his weight.

"Th—Thank you, young man," he gasped as his rescuer eased him upwards.

"Mister," replied a most unmasculine voice, "happen you think I'm a young *man*, they either damaged you real bad, or you've not been around very much."

Even before the lack of masculinity in the voice registered on St. Andre's pain-slowed mind, he rested his hand for support under the jacket and on the shirt below. He jerked the hand away much quicker than he placed it on, for, slowed by the beating or not, St. Andre's faculties told him that what he touched, or what lay beneath the shirt he rested his hand on, most certainly did not belong to a young *man*.

"I should think so too," said the voice, showing no embarassment. "You're too stove up and feeble right now to get ideas like *that*."

"I—I—assure you, young lady—," St. Andre began, feeling the girl brace herself as his weight leaned against her. "I—had—no intention—."

"If you had, you're a tougher cuss than I expected to find in New Orleans," the girl answered calmly. "Soon's I've found that feller's gun, we'll get you some place where I can see how much face they've left you. Only I'd sure as hell hate to leave a loaded gun lying where some darned city kid could find it and likely blow his head off, not knowing any better than fool with it."

Gently the girl leaned St. Andre against the wall. Then she turned and walked across the narrow street, scuffling her feet along. One of them struck something which moved and struck the wall with a metallic click. Taking out a match, the girl rasped it on the seat of her pants—for she appeared to be wearing trousers and not a skirt. Bending, her back to St. Andre so he could see little of her features in the faint glow of the burning match, the girl picked up the discarded Derringer. She lowered its hammer before dropping the deadly little single-shot pistol into her jacket pocket. Blowing out the match, the girl turned and walked back to where St. Andre leaned against the other wall.

"Derringer hide-out," she said. "Don't reckon he could've hit me with it. Only I sure as hell didn't aim to stand around and wait to find out. How're you feeling now? Any pain in your side when you breath?"

While watching the girl, St. Andre was feeling at his ribs and wondering just how much damage had been done. His face felt raw and his throat burned with the taste of swallowed blood. A sick fear crept through him as he realised he could not see through his left eye. Weakly he raised a hand to touch it, feeling something wet and sticky. Over the eye lay what felt like a two inch wide, one inch deep cut which trickled blood down. St. Andre hoped that blood from the cut and nothing more caused his left eye's lack of sight. From the way his nose felt, swollen and blocked up, he guessed that it still ran blood and his jaw seemed to be enlarged to twice its normal size. However, while his ribs ached badly, he found he could breath without any of the pain which could spell a broken rib or two.

"I—don't think so," he replied to the girl's question.

Taking the detective's right arm, the girl eased it across her shoulders and braced herself under his weight. The street seemed to be spinning around before St. Andre's eyes and his legs felt as if they had lost their bones. For a moment he thought he would fall, but the girl's strength supported his weight and kept him on his feet.

Born to a society which expected its female side to be fragile, gentle and pampered creatures, St. Andre had seen sufficient of the rest of the world to know that some women had to be strong enough to handle a hard day's work. For all that, the strength of the girl whose timely appearance saved him from serious injury, if not death, took the detective by surprise. If the way she stood up under him be anything to go by, St. Andre figured she must be about as strong a woman as he had ever met.

"How is it?" she asked, making no attempt to move or go down under his weight.

"A—A little better," replied St. Andre as the dizzy feeling left him.

"Happen you're up to it, we'd best get you off the street. Who was they, angry husbands?"

"I—I—."

"Now don't you pay me no mind, nor bothering answering, feller," interrupted the girl. "I'm only doing it to take your mind offen your hurts. I've got me a room around here someplace. Leastways, I reckon it should be around here. Trouble being I didn't blaze no trail and these city streets all look mighty alike to a half-smart lil country gal like me. Where-at's the *Rue de la Paix*?"

While talking, the girl started to walk, assisting St. Andre's still feeble legs to support and carry him. By the time she asked her question about the direction to her temporary home, they had reached the intersection. Although the girl pronounced her street '*Roo dee lah Packs*', St. Andre understood. Weakly he nodded in the direction the girl had been walking before she came to his aid.

"Next street—left," he told her.

"Hell, I wasn't so far wrong after all," she said and stiffened him as he stumbled slightly. "Just keep your legs moving, friend, and lean on me. You can rest up a mite when we get to my room."

Gritting his teeth, and promising himself that he would not throw any more strain than necessary on the girl, St. Andre forced his legs to move. His superb physical condition aided him and the dizziness began to wear off. They walked along the side of a slightly wider street, keeping to the shadows. This latter was the girl's idea although one which St. Andre agreed with in principle.

"Them four riled-up husbands, or fathers, or whatever they was, might come back," she said, steering him into the shadows instead of crossing to where the moon illuminated the other side of the street. "It'd be best if we saw them afore they saw us, I reckon."

After walking for a time, coherent thoughts began to flow into St. Andre's head. While he did not feel like throwing somersaults with joy, or even trying to walk without the girl's aid, he could now think. Being a policeman who had just taken one hell of a beating, his first thoughts turned to his attackers.

The name 'Max' yelled by one of the quartet might possibly

help in locating them, although St. Andre could not even try to guess how many hard-cases in New Orleans went under that name. It would be several decades before any police department maintained more than the most fragmentary records and in the early 1870's the useful idea of keeping a 'monicker' file, which listed criminals by their nicknames had not been thought of, so St. Andre had no such aid to assist his search.

St. Andrew wanted those four men badly and ought to blow his whistle, bringing patrolmen to help him begin his search. Yet in his weakened condition the prospect of being able to get off his feet for a time and have his injuries treated prevented him from doing so. The four attackers would be well clear of the area and St. Andre did not feel up to the task of starting at that moment.

All four men bore marks from his fists and feet, of that he felt sure. From the way they yelled and howled as his rescuer tackled them, the quartet might carry other identifiable injuries too. St. Andre suddenly realised that he did not know just how the girl managed to drive off four burly rough-necks. If it came to a point he knew very little about his saviour. Who she might be; what she looked like; how she came to be on hand; where she came from; all those questions remained unasked as she helped him towards the *Rue de la Paix*.

"This's it," remarked the girl, steering him towards the door of a cheap brownstone apartment building. "We'll have you fit as frog's hair afore you know what it's about."

Opening the door, the girl helped St. Andrew through the dimly-lit hall to a room on the ground floor. She let them into the room and assisted St. Andre across to a bed, sitting him on it then easing him deftly on to his back. Even now St. Andre had seen little of his rescuer for the room was in darkness.

"Just lie easy there, friend," she ordered. "I'll light the lamp and then see to fixing your hurts."

With a sigh, St. Andre relaxed and waited for the lamp to be lit and allow him to take a good look at the girl whose opportune arrival and prompt actions saved him from serious injury.

# CHAPTER TWO

## So You're The Famous Calamity Jane

ALTHOUGH St. Andre did not feel like acting the part of an observant detective, he looked around him as well as he could with only one eye working properly, when the lamp's light illuminated the room. He found himself in a small, clean room furnished with a wash-stand on which stood a pitcher of water and a towel, a small table bearing the lamp, a couple of chairs, a wardrobe and a comfortable bed.

From his rapid study of the room, St. Andrew took his first clear look at his rescuer. Remembering the robust language she used when driving off the quartet, St. Andre half-expected to see a harsh-faced, middle-aged harridan of some kind. He received a very pleasant surprise. Maybe his rescuer could not be termed ravingly beautiful, but she was good looking and well below middle-age.

Most ladies of St. Andre's acquaintance, and there were several, went in for blonde hair that season, whether born blonde or not, wore it long and taken up in elaborate styles; while their faces retained a pallor aided by powder and make-up. His rescuer had a mop of short, curly red hair on which perched a battered U.S. cavalry kepi at a jaunty angle, and her face bore a healthy tan sprinkled with a few attractive freckles. The eyes of most women St. Andre knew were languorous, inviting; yet a man never knew when he accepted the invitation if the girl would submit in blissful delight as he took hold, or scream for her papa to bring on a shotgun and a preacher. That red haired girl's eyes held no hidden deceit. Meeting St. Andre's scrutiny calmly, they seemed to say, "All right, son, hurt or not, you figure you're the world's greatest; but I'm from Missouri, I've got to be shown."

Showing her might prove mighty interesting.

After his study of the girl's face, St. Andre watched her walk across the room. Removing the fringed buckskin jacket she wore, the girl hung it on a wardrobe peg then bent and opened a battered box standing against the wall. A tight-rolled scarlet bandana, knotted at her throat, trailed long ends over an open-necked man's shirt that, like the levis pants she wore, looked to have been bought a size too small and shrunk in the washing. The shirt's neck was open low enough, and clung tight enough to her rich, full bosom, to dispel any doubts that might possibly have remained in St. Andre's French-Creole mind as to her sex. From the bosom, she tapered down to a slim waist, without the use of corsets or other artificial aids, then swelled out to plump, curving and eye-catching hips and shapely legs that the levis tended to reveal rather than conceal, and ended in feet clad in Indian moccasins unless St. Andrew missed his guess.

Lifting his gaze from her feet, St. Andre studied the broad leather belt which slanted down at an angle from her left hip to her right thigh. Surely she did not wear a gun? Yes, it showed as she turned from the box. An ivory-handled 1861 Navy Colt, butt forward in a contoured fast-draw holster such as members of the Texas Light Cavalry wore during the War Between the States, or St. Andre missed his guess; the holster bottom fastened down by a thong around the girl's thigh. An affectation if ever he saw one, probably the girl had been on her way to a masquerade ball when she found him in need of her aid. A long lashed bull-whip hung thrust into the left side of her waist belt. More affectation—at that moment St. Andre remembered the pistol-like cracks and the pain-filled howls of his attackers as the girl drove them off. That whip was no affectation, no matter what the gunbelt and Navy Colt might be.

"Damned if everything you want's allus at the bottom," she remarked and swung back to root in the box again, a few muttered curses leaving her lips.

St. Andrew found himself wondering what kind of girl he had come across. She was refreshingly different from his aristocratic and socialite friends, or the actresses and other entertainers he knew or met in his duty. Some of the young ladies of St. Andre's social set, profound admirers of the intellectual writer Browne Crossman used bad language to express their progressiveness; but they did it self-consciously, showing only that they tried to prove a non-existent point. The red head cursed naturally, in the manner of a man out fishing when he caught his thumb with a hook point. St. Andre grinned as he thought of the vitriolic flow of invective the girl poured upon his attackers while her savage whip-attack drove them off.

"You should tote a gun, friend, happen those were your neighbours," the girl said, coming to the bed with a buckskin bag in her hands. "Sit up and let's take a look at you."

Gently, yet showing that she had handled injured men before, she helped him sit up and remove his jacket. Her eyes studied him and formed their conclusions. While he did not look much right at the moment, mussed up and all bloody, she decided he would be a handsome cuss most times. Black curly hair, regular features, a neat, thin moustache; wearing expensive clothing and looking like he was used to doing so, but with a good spread to his shoulders, a lean, fighting man's waist and, if the way he fought those four jaspers be anything to go on, hard muscles that he knew how to use. In fact, he looked a tolerable hunk of man to her way of thinking.

"I—have—a—gun." St. Andre replied.

"Then why in hell didn't you start to using it?" she sniffed, swinging the jacket on to the bed rail.

Something hard clinked against the rail and the girl turned, dipping a hand into his inside pocket to lift out a fancy, pearl-handled Smith & Wesson No. 1 Pocket revolver which she eyed with distaste. Yet she did not shriek in simulated horror and drop the gun, or wave it around with a finger on the trigger to the danger of life and limb. Handling the gun with obvious knowledge of such things, she turned smiling eyes to him.

"See now why you didn't use it," she said and laid the revolver aside. "Reckon you didn't want to knock the dust off their jackets."

Despite his injuries, St. Andre was still a Frenchman in the presence of a pretty girl and as such figured it to be time he asserted some of his masculine superiority over that calm, competent young female.

"It would have done more than just dust a jacket, *cherie*," he told her, sniffing the dripping blood up his nostrils.

"Maybe," she answered, sounding doubtful. "The name's not 'Sherry', it's Martha Jane Canary, though I'd not thank you for calling me 'Martha'."

"Then what do I call you?"

"My friends call me Calam, or worse. Which, afore you ask me, is short for Calamity."

While speaking, the girl had opened her bag and taken out what looked like a powderhorn, tipping some snuff-like grains of dust on to the palm of her hand. Turning, she approached St. Andre and held the hand towards him.

"Here, sniff some of this up your nose."

"Huh?"

"Could allus call in one of them fancy city doctors and he'd look

18

you over then tell you what we both already know, that somebody handed you a helluva licking, and charge you five dollars. Only I like to do it more gentle and cheaper."

So saying, the girl brought the palm of her hand up under his nose and stabbed her other forefinger hard into his stomach. Taken by surprise, St. Andre breathed in, sucking a quantity of the powder up into his nostrils. For a moment his nose felt clogged up, but the bleeding stopped.

"What was that?" he asked, watching the girl put away the powder and open a large snuff box.

"Powdered witch hazel leaves. And this here's gum from a balsam fir. I reckon it's better for stopping open bleeding like this on your face. This might hurt a mite, friend."

She went to the washstand and poured water from the jug into a bowl. Returning with the bowl and towel, she gently washed the blood from his injured eye. For a moment St. Andre felt scared as he saw the concern show on her face, then relief replaced the expression of anxiety.

"Calamity you said your name was," the detective said, trying to ignore the stinging pain the bathing caused. "Well, it nearly was a calamity. The life of New Orleans' best detective might have been cut off in his prime had you not come along when you did."

"Was there two of you in the alley?" asked the girl with a smile. She spread something cool and sticky on the gash over his eye.

"Only one. I, myself."

"And you'd be who?"

"Philippe St. Andre, Detective Lieutenant, at your service."

"Right pleased to know you. Might not be seeing too good out of that eye for a spell, but at least you've got an eye left and the cut over it don't need any stitching."

"I suppose you could have done that too?"

"I've had to afore now," the girl admitted. "Stop the pain by making 'em chew on the bark of a pepperwood tree, if there's one handy. If not, I've got a couple of other real good pain-killers. One of 'em's make the hurt feller drink whisky until he goes to sleep——."

"I'd imagine that would cause him to cut himself again when he woke, to get the same treatment," St. Andre interrupted.

"If it does, I use the other pain-killer next time."

"And what might that be?"

"Hit him over the head with the empty bottle," she answered calmly, then eyed him with interest. "Ain't never been a gal for being nosey and asking questions about things, so I'm not going to ask you if them four *was* riled-up fathers after your hide."

"*Mon Dieu!* I forgot them, *cherie*."

"Likely they'll not forget *you* for a spell. Shouldn't be hard to cut from the herd, happen you look for the marks that old whip of mine put on 'em. One'll have a busted wrist most likely and the others'll all carry marks."

"You're quite a girl to have around in a calamity, Jane," smiled St. Andre, then he stiffened and stared at the girl, realising how the last two words came out. "Calamity—Jane—You can't be!"

"Want to bet?" she grinned back.

"*Sacre bleu!*" St. Andre ejaculated. "So you're the famous Calamity Jane!"

"Yep," replied the girl, clearly just a mite proud that her name and fame had reached as far as New Orleans. "I'm the famous Calamity Jane. Only I didn't know I was famous down here in New Orleans."

St. Andre stared in fascination at the girl he previously believed to be no more than a legend created by Westerners for the purpose of joshing dudes. Many highly sensational tales of her adventures, prowess and capabilities had appeared over the last year in such magazines as the *Police Gazette* and *New York Ledger*; in fact even the sedate *New Orleans Picayune* occasionally carried stories concerning the life and times of Calamity Jane.

In the highly coloured stories St. Andre read, Calamity had been portrayed as either a fire-breathing middle-aged dragoness, or a ravingly beautiful woman of high birth who fled to the West to forget a lost lover. Calamity was neither, but merely a rather unusual product of the times. Before disappearing into the West, Charlotte Canary left Calamity and the rest of her children in the care of a St. Louis convent. However, there had been too much of Charlotte's spirit in Calamity for the girl to accept the nuns' rigid discipline. On her sixteenth birthday, Calamity—then plain Martha Jane—hid in one of Dobe Killem's wagons and was not discovered until that evening at the end of a day's trip. She might have been returned to the convent had Killem's cook not been too drunk to make a meal for the men. One of the few things the nuns managed to teach Calamity had been cooking and the meal she threw together for the hungry men ensured that she could stay with the outfit.

That trip raiding Sioux wiped out two other outfits, but missed Killem's wagons. On reaching their destination, Killem made a good profit and his men began to regard the girl as a good luck charm. So they kept her with them. At first Calamity helped the cook, did chores around the camp, then graduated to driving. From the men she learned to handle a six-horse Conestoga wagon, use a bull-whip as tool and weapon, shoot well with rifle, revolver or shotgun, and generally take care of herself on the plains country of the West. Due to a licking at the hands of a saloon girl, Calamity learned to fight. More than that, she developed a liking for fighting which led her to enter saloons and toss down a challenge to take on the best gal in the house, all-in hand-scalping with no holds barred. Her outfit picked up a fair amount of cash betting on her, for so far Calamity had never been beaten in a fight.

St. Andre knew none of this. All he saw was a merry-faced, competent and capable girl, unconventional perhaps and well outside his considerable knowledge of the opposite sex. She reminded him of the fresh-faced, buxom country girls one saw around the poorer section of the city; wholesome, naive, innocent —only he doubted if Calamity would prove all that innocent if things came to a head.

"How about your ribs?" she asked.

"I think they'll be all right," he replied, feeling suddenly shy and not doubting she would want to examine his torso should he claim different. So he changed the subject. "What brought you to New Orleans?"

"Somebody in the Army bought up a big bunch of horses cheap down here and wanted 'em shipping up the Big Muddy to St. Jo. So they sent for Dobe Killem, he's my boss, to handle the collection and delivery. We come down by steamboat and here we are. I went out to see the sights just afore dark and got lost coming back. Reckon the boys've gone off to that Madam Darcel's place and want me to meet 'em there."

"Madam Darcel's—," gasped St. Andre. "You mean the *Cheval D'Or?*"

"Yep. Though what the hell a 'Shovel Door' is, I ain't figured out."

"*Cheval D'Or,*" corrected the detective. "It means Golden Horse. But it's no place for a young lady."

"Happen I see any going in," grinned Calamity, "I'll warn 'em."

Knowing something of Madam Darcel's saloon, St. Andre felt he ought to give a further warning.

"I owe you my gratitude for saving me, Miss—,"

"Happen you want to show that gratitude," she interrupted,

"stop calling me 'Miss' and start saying 'Calam', or Jane, or even that there 'Sherry'. And don't go to fretting. The boys protect me—and I protect them."

"Is any of the boys your—," began St. Andre, then tapered off, not knowing how to finish his question.

"Nope. None of 'em's my 'your—'. They're like a bunch of big brothers to me. Reckon I'll go on out and find em."

'Unless you have other ideas,' her manner hinted.

St. Andre, as has been said, was a Frenchman, a lusty healthy young man with an eye for the ladies and a heart that took kindly to romance. Unfortunately he was also a policeman responsible for keeping the peace and investigating crimes. The peace had been broken and a crime committed, which meant he must put duty before what he felt sure would be a pleasure.

"I must also go out and try to find somebody, *cherie*," he said regretfully, and waited for an explosion. No girl liked having *that* kind of offer tossed aside.

"Them four?" she asked calmly; perhaps the calm before a breaking storm.

"Those four," he agreed. "There are questions I must ask them."

"I figured there might be," Calamity stated showing neither disappointment nor annoyance, only complete understanding. "A good lawman can't let anybody get away with working him over. It gives other folks wrong ideas and puts bad medicine in 'em."

"Who told you that?" asked the detective in surprise.

"The best danged man who ever wore a law-badge—west of the Mississippi that is."

"And who would that be, Wyatt Earp?"

"That fighting pimp?" scoffed Calamity. "I'm talking about a real man. You maybe heard of him. Dusty Fog."

"You *know* Captain Fog?" asked the impressed St. Andre, for the man named had been one of the most talked-about soldiers in the Confederate States cavalry and much in the news since the meeting at the Appomattox Court-House brought an end to military hostilities.*

"Met him a couple of times," Calamity admitted. "Know his pard, Mark Counter a whole heap better."†

"I also met Captain Fog, during the War when I rode with the

---

*Dusty Fog's adventures are told in J. T. Edson's Floating Outfit novels.
†Calamity's meetings with Mark Counter are recorded in THE WILDCATS and TROUBLED RANGE.

Greyson Daredevils. He was a fine soldier and correct about a lawman's duty."

"Old Dusty gets right about more things than any two fellas I know," answered Calamity. "Say, did you ever see the fancy way he fist-fights? That's sure something to see."

"You are right," agreed St. Andre. "He uses a unique method. I wish I knew half as much. Of course I know *savate*—."

"What the hell's that?" asked the girl, packing away her medicines in the buckskin bag.

"*Savate?* French foot-fighting. It was brought to perfection by a man called Michel in Paris, France. I learned at Duval's academy and he studied in Paris under Charles Lecour, Michel's star pupil."

"Must be real fancy, taking all that learning," Calamity said dryly. "I can kick real good and never took a lesson in my sinful young life."

"Ah, *cherie*, there is kicking and—*la savate*. Perhaps during your stay in our fair city I might be permitted to take you to Duval's and show you how *savate* is learned."

"Allus willing to learn something," the girl replied and took the bag to her small trunk.

Although she did not know it, Calamity was due for a lesson in the noble art of *savate* a whole heap sooner than she expected. Her main thought-line at the moment of stowing away the medicine bag was that she would be seeing that fancy-talking, handsome young feller again. Now that might be *real* interesting.

Reaching up his hand, St. Andre touched the cut over his left eye. The blood, assisted by the gum, had congealed and the groove felt much smaller than when he previously examined it. One thing brought relief to the detective. Although the vision was blurred, he could still see and the damage to the eye appeared to be only to the lids and surrounding area. He wondered if a doctor could have handled his injuries any more efficiently than had the girl.

"How'd you like me to see if I can raise a cup of coffee?" Calamity asked as she returned from the box.

It was a tempting prospect for St. Andre, as he had not yet thrown off all the effects of the beating. However he wished to make a start on the hunt for his attackers before his injuries began to stiffen up. He knew that the longer it took him to start, the harder commencing would be. So, although his body craved to stay relaxed on the comfortable bed, he declined the offer.

"Perhaps another time, *cherie*," he replied, rising from the bed and reaching for his coat. "Now I must go down town and start work."

"Reckon I'd rather have a snort of red-eye myself," Calamity admitted. "How do I find the 'Shovel Door'?"

"It is on Latour Street. As a matter of fact, I intend to start my inquiries from the Latour Street station house. If you wish, I'll ride over there with you. We can hire a carriage."

"You know the range and I don't. Hey, aren't you forgetting something?"

Having put on his jacket, St. Andre started to walk towards the door of the room, but the girl's last words brought him to a halt. He turned and looked at her, but her eyes were not on him. Following Calamity's gaze, he saw his gun lying where the girl laid it aside.

"Oh that," he said. "I suppose I'd better take it with me."

A frown creased Calamity's face as she watched St. Andre drop the Smith & Wesson into his jacket pocket. No Western lawman would have left his weapon behind. One might forget his hat, or possibly his pants, but never his gun. Come to that, no Western peace officer would straddle himself with such a puny, feeble revolver as a .22 calibre Smith & Wesson. While that handsome young cuss might be real smart in some ways, it was Calamity's considered opinion that he had a lot to learn about being a lawman.

Not wishing to create dissension, Calamity did not mention her thoughts. She drew on her buckskin jacket, decided that she would not need her bull whip again that night and went to blow out the lamp. Then she left the room on St. Andre's arm, acting for all the world like a for-real New Orleans' lady. Or as near one as wearing man's clothing and with a Navy Colt hung at her right hip would allow.

# CHAPTER THREE

## *Miss Canary Walks In The Park*

WHILE Calamity never felt really comfortable riding in a vehicle with somebody else at the ribbons, she found the one-horse carriage they hired to take them to Latour Street had its advantages. Sitting inside, without the worry of keeping the horse going, Calamity relaxed and St. Andre pointed out various places of interest as they rode. At last they came alongside the large, open space known as the City Park, and the detective waved his hand towards it.

"Latour Street is on the other side of the Park. But we will have to go around it to reach the *Cheval D'Or*."

A saloon girl who Calamity once fought with, beat, then befriended, had come from New Orleans and in the course of a conversation mentioned taking walks in City Park. From what the girl said, walking there had a special appeal and Calamity decided she might as well give it a whirl while so close.

"Reckon I'll save the horses some sweat," she remarked, "Tell the feller up there to stop and I'll walk across."

"You mean you wish to walk through the Park alone, and at night?" asked St. Andre, staring at the girl.

"Won't be going to the 'Shovel Door' in the morning, so it'll have to be tonight. Only I don't reckon you're feeling like walking, so I'll be alone."

"*Mon Dieu!* Haven't you heard of the Strangler?"

"Nope. Who's he?"

"I wish we knew. All we know is that he has killed seven girls in the Park."

If St. Andre hoped to frighten or shock Calamity, he appeared to fail badly. Not by a flicker of her face did she show any fear or concern. However, her right hand dropped under the side of her jacket and touched the butt of the Navy Colt.

"I'm dressed," she said quietly. "Stop the carriage, Sherry, and I'll take me a walk."

St. Andre did not understand the connotation behind a Westerner's statement about being dressed. It had nothing to do with the fact that the speaker wore all his, or her, clothing, but implied that the one who made the statement carried the most important article of West-country property, a gun.

One thing St. Andre did not know, even after a short acquaintance; once Calamity made up her mind, very little under the sun would cause her to change it. However he could not allow a girl, even one so competent as Calamity, to chance walking alone in the park after dark, even on a bright moon-light night.

"If you are determined," he said, "I'll walk with you. And a lady does not call a gentleman '*cherie*'."

"So who's a lady?" grinned Calamity. "Reckon you can stand up to the walk?"

"I'll try my best," St. Andre answered and tapped on the roof of the cab.

Dismounting and helping Calamity down, St. Andre paid off the driver. Then he took Calamity's arm and they walked through the big, wrought iron gates into City Park. Even in the early 1870's New Orleans possessed a really fine park, although under the present conditions various senior police officials wished that the area had been built over instead of used as a recreation spot.

The Park might have been designed with the needs of the Strangler in mind, St. Andre decided, not for the first time, as he and Calamity strolled along. Winding paths ran through clumps of bushes which effectively hid one from the next. Scattered little wooden shelters offered places where courting couples could rest and do the kind of things they had done since men threw away clubs in favour of more gentle and pleasant methods of snaring a pretty young maiden. In that tangle, a man-made jungle-like maze, the Strangler could stalk his prey, slip his killing cord around a slim, delicate female throat and silently add another victim to his growing list, then be gone before the body was found.

So thought Philippe St. Andre, detective lieutenant, as he walked along keeping to the grass verge alongside the path. He hated to make a noise as he walked and so always tried to stay somewhere that muffled his footsteps. At his side, Calamity's moccasins fell silently on the path. Neither spoke as they walked, each busy on his or her line of thought.

In Calamity's case, the thoughts ran to the fun she would soon be having with the boys and wondering what a big city saloon offered in comparison with a similar place out West. She also wondered if the city detective meant his invitation to visit the *savate* academy. If so, how much further would their friendship develop? Calamity had no objections to the friendship blossoming, for, from what she heard, those French-Creole fellers were sure something at handing out the things a girl dreamed about on the long, dark, cold and lonely winter nights.

While passing across a joining with another path, Calamity saw something from the corner of her eye. Even at such a moment, the girl's instincts were to keep alert, so she turned her head to look more carefully at what attracted her. What she saw brought her to a halt and made her tighten her grip on the detective's sleeve.

"Don't make a sound!" she hissed. "Down there!"

The very intensity with which Calamity spoke forced St. Andre to obey in silence. Turning to look in the direction Calamity pointed, St. Andre felt as if his eyes would pop out of his head at the sight before him. If the sight meant what he believed it did, St. Andre figured himself to be having more luck than even the youngest and most handsome lieutenant of the New Orleans Police Department rated.

In pre-Strangler days the sight of a man standing behind a girl in the City Park would have attracted no attention. Yet seeing such a sight now aroused any right-thinking policeman's suspicions. The man stood with his back to Calamity and St. Andre, was medium sized, portly, wearing a top hat, stylishly-cut broadcloth coat, white trousers, the new-fangled spats that had become all the rage, and shiny shoes. Ahead of him, also with her back to the watching couple, stood a buxom, blonde, flashily-dressed girl who most probably was not his lady wife, and likely could not even claim to be a lady. Such a sight had never been so rare in the Park as to attract more than a glance, a cynical grin and some conjecture about how much the girl would make—until the Strangler started operations. Since the killings began however, the sight of a man standing behind a girl and dropping something over her head demanded not only a second glance, but instant action.

Despite his injuries, St. Andre found that he could still think fast. Even as the portly man's hands came level with the girl's throat, the detective let out a yell.

"Police here! Let go and stand still!"

Jerking his head around, the portly man gave a startled squawk. Thrusting the girl aside, he started to run away as fast as his legs would carry him. Ahead lay a corner and once round it he could disappear in any of a dozen directions, or hide in the bushes.

St Andre knew that as did the fleeing man, so sprang forward in pursuit, ignoring the screeching blonde who had landed on hands and knees at the side of the path.

Even as St. Andre leapt forward, Calamity also acted and showed a classic example of the difference between Eastern and Western thought on how to deal with such a problem. St. Andre hoped to run the man down in a foot-race, or at least keep him in sight until reinforcements arrived and cut off his escape. Although the detective carried a fully loaded revolver—even if only a tiny .22 Smith & Wesson—he did not give the weapon a thought, regarding it only as a means of extreme self-defence.

Not so Calamity. Raised on the Western plains, friend of numerous fast and handy gun-fighting gentlemen, she knew the value of a revolver in the present situation. Once around that corner, the man might escape and, if he should be the Strangler, stay free to kill again.

Twisting the palm of her right hand outwards, Calamity curled her fingers around the butt of the Navy Colt and brought it out fairly fast. By Western standards 'fast' meant to be able to draw a gun and shoot in at most three-quarters of a second and Calamity took a quarter of a second longer than that to bring her Colt into action. However, to draw and shoot in a second still licked the 'be-jeesus' out of running when it came to halting a fleeing criminal. Taking careful aim, for she had heard that these civilised areas did not take kindly to having dead owlhoots scattered about the scenery, Calamity fired. On the crack of the shot, the man's tophat somersaulted from his head and bounced on the path ahead of him, although it must be stated that Calamity did not intend to come that close.

Never one to look a gift horse—or a real lucky shot—in the mouth, Calamity acted just like she always hit her mark in so spectacular fashion.

"Hold it!" she yelled. "Stop, or the next one goes clear through you."

Which, with a touch of dramatics—Calamity could never resist a chance to play the grandstand a mite, even though she had never heard of the term—brought about the desired result. However, for a moment Calamity thought a second shot, this time for effect, might be needed. Then the man skidded to a halt, turned and jerked his hands into the air.

"D—Don't shoot!" he quavered. "I—I—only have a few dollars and my watch on me.'

"Well dog—my—cats!" Calamity growled, thumb-cocking

her Colt. "He's trying to make out like he thinks we're fixing to rob him."

"Or he really thinks so," St. Andre answered, for he could not see the Strangler, with only the gallows waiting, surrendering so easily. "Holster your gun, Calam, we won't need it any more."

Figuring that a man who forgot to put his weapon into a pocket before leaving a room could hardly set himself up as an authority on when a gun would be needed, Calamity retained hold of the Colt and kept it from leather.

"I'll believe that when I'm sure of it," she answered.

"Hey!" yelped the gaudily-dressed girl, struggling to her feet and clapping a hand to her throat. "You fellers wouldn't ta—My pearls!" The last two words came in a wild screech. "They must have bust when he pushed me. You lousy bastards made me lose my pearls!"

At the same moment the portly man came forward on shaking legs. He reached under his jacket, causing Calamity to prepare to shoot. However, she held her hand for something told her the man was harmless. In fact from the front he showed what would normally be a florid, pompous face, yet which now held a pale, terrified expression as befitted a very respectable member of society believing himself to be under a threat to his life and well-being. Nothing more dangerous than a well-filled wallet came from his jacket front and he held it forward timidly.

"H—Here!" he squeaked. "T—Take my wallet—."

"You yeller crumb!" screeched the girl. "Do something! They made me lose the pearls you just gave me."

"All right!" snapped St. Andre, walking by Calamity. "I'm a police lieutenant. Let's be quiet and talk this out."

While the detective's cold, authoritative voice chopped off the girl's indignation, it brought a change of attitude in the portly man. The fear went and he thrust away his wallet with an angry gesture. Righteous anger came to his pompous features as he pointed at St. Andre and Calamity.

"Police!" he snorted. "Then why did you shoot at me?" Without giving either the detective or Calamity a chance to answer, he went on, "I'll have you know that I'm a personal friend of the Mayor and the Chief of Police—."

"Your sort allus are," sniffed Calamity, setting the Colt's hammer on a safety notch between two cap-nipples and twirling the gun into leather with a fancy flourish.

"What did you say?" boomed the now fully indignant citizen. "I'll have you know, my good man—."

"I ain't good, I for certain ain't your'n, and I sure as hell ain't no man, mister!" growled Calamity, listening to the sound of heavy, official feet pounding along a path towards them. "We saw you stood behind that gal and tossing something over her head—."

"It was a string of pearls!" howled the blonde, down on her hands and knees and scrabbling around with her fingers. "Light a match, one of you and get down to help me find 'em. They cost him a hundred bucks and he gave them to me instead of paying."

Which cleared in a most satisfactory manner the matter of why the man stood behind the girl and acted as he did; although St. Andre knew enough about tax-paying citizens of the portly man's type to doubt if the pompous one would be pleased to hear somebody took him for the Strangler. There would be stormy times ahead unless St. Andre handled the business just right, and the blonde's words offered him a reasonably good way of dealing with the pompous man.

"Hum!" said St. Andre, nudging Calamity in the ribs gently as a warning for her to let him handle the matter. "A hundred dollar pearl necklace lost. That's a serious affair, sir. I'll have to ask you to come along to the nearest station house and make a full statement."

At that moment a couple of burly policemen came into sight, skidding to a halt and studying the group before them. Then one of the patrolmen recognised St. Andre and threw up a salute.

"Heard a shot down here, lootenant," he said.

"Er—Lieutenant," the portly man put in, his voice no longer pompous or indignant as he considered his position in the light of St. Andre's words. "Do we have to go on with this?"

"With the loss of a hundred dollar necklace, on top of your being shot at?" answered St. Andre. "I think we must."

Gulping down something which seemed to be blocking his throat, the portly man held out a hand. "I—I understand that you and this—this—you misjudged my intentions. The whole affair was no more than a regrettable error and should be forgotten, don't you think?"

"And the pearls, sir?"

"The—They were not that valuable, lieutenant. You look like a man of the world—."

"What was their true value?" interrupted St. Andre coldly.

"A—Two dollars fifty. They were freshwater pearls."

"*What!*" screeched the girl, coming to her feet with fury showing on her face. "Why, you cheap, mealy-mouthed—."

"Now you just quieten it down, Sally," put in one of the patrolmen.

"Me?" yelped the girl. "And what about him? He gave me them to—."

"Likely," said the patrolman. "You'd—."

"That's it!" the blonde screamed. "Side him! It's like Browne Crossman is always saying, you lousy police are just tools of the rich and—."

At which point Miss Martha Jane Canary decided it was time she took a hand. Not having received the benefit of a college education, Calamity felt respect and admiration for most lawmen, knowing the thankless job they did. So she disliked seeing folks call down a peace officer without having a damned good reason.

Shooting out a hand, Calamity gripped the other girl's dress, sliding fingers between the valley of the girl's breasts and taking a firm hold of the material. With a sudden jerk, she hauled the blonde up close and thrust an angry face within inches of the other girl's startled features.

"Now shut your god-damned mouth and listen to me, you cat-house cull!" yelled Calamity and when that girl raised her voice, man you could hear it for a good country mile. "We saw you in what we reckoned looked like danger of winding up wolf-bait, so we jumped in and saved you. Only it come out you didn't need saving after all. And if you're so damned dumb that you fall for an old-as-the-hills trick like the pearl game, you've got no cause, nor right, to complain."

While Calamity never followed the other girl's profession, she possessed a number of good friends who did, so knew enough about it to talk to the blonde in terms they both could understand. Her angry tirade stopped the blonde's speech describing Browne Crossman's views on the position of law officers as tools of the idle rich and oppressors of the poor.

Anger glowed in the blonde's eyes at first, then died again. The two patrolmen knew something of the girl's temper and expected her to tie into the red-head in a hair-yanking, nail-clawing brawl. In this expectation they did the blonde an injustice. Full of righteous indignation she might be; a rough girl in a tough trade she most certainly was; but she had enough sense to think before acting. Taking note of Calamity's free hand and seeing it folded into a useful-looking fist, remembering the strength behind the other girl's pull, and figuring that anybody who knew enough about her work to mention the 'pearl game' must also know other basic essentials like self-defence, the blonde decided not to take

31

the matter further. If she tangled with that girl in men's clothing, her every instinct warned her she might regret the decision. There was too much competition for customers without operating under the added disadvantage of sporting a fight-battered face. So the girl relapsed into sullen silence, contenting herself with throwing a malevolent glare at the portly man.

Watching Calamity release the blonde, St. Andre fought to hold down a grin. It seemed the young lady from the West had good answers to most of the world's problems. However, there was the matter on hand to be attended to before he could compliment Calamity on her numerous talents.

"Do you want to take the matter further, sir?" asked St. Andre, eyeing the portly man in his most chilling and authoritative manner.

Under other conditions the man might have liked to show his tax-paying superiority over the three public-servants whose salary he helped pay. But not when he could be taken to the police station house and maybe word of his escapade get out. Unfortunately for him, 'making an investigation for social reasons' had not yet been invented as an excuse for his proposed conduct—and anyhow his wife would never have believed it—so he decided to keep quiet and get away while the getting be good and still open.

"No. I realise it was all a simple mistake," he said magnanimously. "If you don't mind, gentlemen, I think I'll be on my way."

Turning, the man scuttled off at a fair speed, ignoring his bullet-holed tophat which still lay where it fell. The blonde watched him go, then gave an explosive and angry snort.

"Why that—!" she began.

"Call it one of the hazards of your trade, my pet," St. Andre interrupted. They stood listening to the rapidly departing patter of the man's feet for a moment, then the detective went on, "But I wouldn't advise you to go into the Park with strange men in future."

Strange as it may seem, the blonde had never thought about the Strangler when she accepted the portly man's invitation to take a walk in the Park prior to visiting her room and getting down to business. Nor could she think of a single good reason why she should not take advantage of the civic amenities to put her clients in a romantic mood which tended to make them open their pocket-books all the wider when paying for her services.

"Why not?" she asked.

Before any answer could be made, a horror-filled male scream rang out from the direction in which the portly man took his hurried departure. It rang out loud, drowning the faint, but ever-present noise of merry-making from Latour Street. So hideous and shocking was the sound that it froze the three men and two girls for an instant. Calamity recovered first, or maybe the drawing of the Navy Colt was no more than reflex action. All three police-men stared in the direction of the sound and the blonde's face lost its colour as her mouth dropped open.

"What was that?" she finally gasped.

Her words bounced off departing backs as Calamity and the three men went racing away in the direction of the scream.

"It could be the answer to your question," Calamity called back over her shoulder as she ran.

For a moment the blonde stood staring. Then she remembered the Strangler and realised why St. Andre and Calamity acted as they did on seeing her standing before her prospective client as he slipped the string of freshwater pearls around her neck. Suddenly she saw that the departure of the police left her alone and a feeling of terror hit her.

"Wait for me!" she screeched and fled after the others as fast as she could run.

# CHAPTER FOUR

## *Miss Canary Sees A Strangler Victim*

CROUCHING hidden among the bushes at the side of the track the Strangler let out a low hiss of annoyance as he watched the blonde's hurried departure on the heels of the rest of the running group.

While making his way out of City Park after killing his eighth victim, the Strangler had come on the sight of the portly man and the blonde. Deciding it would be both interesting and amusing to watch what happened, the Strangler crouched in the bushes and awaited developments. The developments came swiftly with the arrival of that damned aristocratic St. Andre and the girl wearing men's clothing of an outlandish cut and style such as one saw Westerners clad in. Much to the Strangler's amusement, St. Andre took the portly man's actions as being an attempt to strangle the blonde.

Then the Strangler's amusement died as the girl with St. Andre swiftly—the move looked amazingly fast to the Strangler's untutored eyes—drew a revolver from under her coat and shot the fleeing man's hat from his head. The Strangler had often heard of Westerners drawing and shooting their weapons in lightning fast moves but as *he* could not do so, doubted if any less intelligent person would be able to perform the feat. Having seen the girl with St. Andre draw and shoot, the Strangler began to wonder if he might possibly have been wrong. If her clothes be anything to go by, the red haired girl came from the Western plains country, and the Strangler had never seen anything so fast as the way she moved.

Thinking of the girl's speed made the Strangler freeze in his hiding place instead of sneaking off and escaping. If he tried to flee and made a noise, that girl might start shooting at him. To the Strangler's way of thinking, his life's work was too important for him to risk capture and hanging because he killed a few worthless girls with so little to offer the community. So he remained crouching in the bushes and watched the smooth manner in which St. Andre handled the righteous indignation of the portly citizen. Being born to riches, St. Andre ought not have shown such efficiency, but he invariably did as the Strangler well knew; and the Strangler hated the thought of his preconceived ideas of aristocratic behaviour being shattered.

The Strangler thought the affair must be over when the portly man departed, and that he would soon be able to leave the area in safety. On hearing the man's scream, the Strangler knew his latest victim's body had been found. As the Strangler watched the rapid departure of the three policemen and the Western girl, he had an idea. Why not kill that gaudily-dressed blonde? If word came out that he took a second victim in such a manner, St. Andre would be dismissed and the people's faith in the police further diminish.

Even as he slid the cord from his pocket, the Strangler savoured the thought of what to do. Maybe the girl would hear him, but her kind never mistrusted *him*. She would think nothing of his presence; they never did. Then the cord would be around her throat from behind, tightening, driving the three knots into flesh and cutting off her voice, turning, he would carry the cord up over his shoulder until they stood back to back and he could use the extra leverage to speed her death.

Only before he could step from the bushes, the girl fled after the departing party. Giving a sigh, the Strangler coiled the length of cord and dropped it into the large pocket of his jacket. He threw a disappointed glance after the fleeing blonde, then walked on to the path and away. His route would take him out of City Park in the direction of the old French Quarter, the upper-crust section of the city.

Not knowing how close they had been to the Strangler, Calamity and the three policemen ran swiftly along the tracks. Despite his earlier beating, St. Andre made good time and he alone kept pace with Calamity as she sped along. The girl did not run with the exaggerated hip-wagglings and arm wavings of most of her sex, but strode out like a man and covered ground fast in her moccasined feet. Behind Calamity and St. Andre came the patrolmen, their uniforms and heavy boots not making for speed of foot; and in the rear staggered a scared, gasping blonde street-walker, the least used to running of them all.

Rounding a corner, Calamity and St. Andre came face to face with the portly, though no longer pompous man. Instead he looked almost on the verge of collapse, face white and drawn in an expression of extreme horror, eyes staring and mouth open, muttering incoherently as he pointed behind him.

"B—b—b—ba—there!" he gasped. "Its'—I—She—I—."

Which told Calamity and the detective little or nothing, but all they needed to know. Thrusting by the portly man, Calamity started to move towards that crumpled heaped-up thing lying in the centre of the path. St. Andre also passed the portly man, who had never been more pleased to see human faces and police uniforms in all his life. Catching Calamity by the arm, St. Andre stopped her. Once again St. Andre tried to assert his inborn French superiority over a member of the weaker sex. After all, and despite her smooth efficiency in practical matters, Calamity *was* a woman—and St. Andre knew just how terrible a Strangler's victim looked.

"Let me," he said.

He went by Calamity and walked towards the shape on the path, fighting to keep his stomach from heaving at the thought of what he would see. Even as he dropped to one knee by the body, St. Andre heard a soft foot-fall beside him and a low feminine gasp. He realised that Calamity had ignored his advice.

In the course of her life as a freighter on the Great Plains, Calamity had seen a fair amount of death: from Indian arrow, war lance or scalping knife; by bullets; through illness and accident. She reckoned to have a stout stomach which no sight could trouble any more. Yet for all that Calamity felt sick as she looked down on the moon-light illuminated features of the Strangler's eighth victim. She sucked in a deep breath and let it out in a slow hiss of revulsion and anger.

The cord which ended the victim's life no longer coiled around her neck, but a livid mark on the pallid skin and indented deeply into the flesh showed where it passed around and tightened, choking off life-giving air and killing far more silently yet just as efficiently as any bullet. Maybe in life the victim had been a beautiful girl, there was no way of knowing from her hideously distorted features now purplish-black, the tongue protruding through open lips and the eyes bulging out of the head. The body, clad in the cheap finery of a street girl, looked good, rich, full and inviting—unless one also looked at the face.

Even the two patrolmen, not sensitive, highly strung or easily moved by scenes of violence, showed nausea at the sight. One of them let out a low curse and the other, slightly younger, turned his head to look away from the hideous thing which had so recently been a living, breathing, happy and maybe good-looking girl.

"Is this the Strangler's work?" asked Calamity, her voice hoarse and strained and her tanned face pale.

"His eighth victim," answered St. Andre bitterly, looking at the three deeper indentations in the flesh, signs of the special type of cord the Strangler always used.

"Maybe he's still around!" snarled the younger patrolman and started moving towards the bushes.

"Hold it, friend!" snapped Calamity, an idea coming to her.

The urgency in Calamity's voice brought the man to a halt and he looked at her. So far nobody had got around to explaining who that girl in men's clothing might be, but she appeared to be on amiable terms with St. Andre, and it did not pay a young patrolman to ignore or give offence to the friends, especially lady friends, of a lieutenant; particularly a lieutenant tipped to wind up as Chief of Police one day in the future.

"What's up, ma'am?" asked the patrolman, sounding more polite than usual.

"He's long gone and you couldn't find him in the bushes at night, so don't go tramping all over the sign. Comes morning I can get a feller here as can track a bird through the air—."

"If you mean follow the Strangler's tracks, Calam, it won't work," St. Andre interrupted. "We tried it with bloodhounds and got nowhere."

"Which same don't surprise me none," the girl answered. "I bet every time a gal's been found, your fellers started chasing around in the bushes looking for the jasper who done it, going every damned which-ways and getting no place 'cept all over the Strangler's tracks. Then there's the folks who use the Park each day, they walk about in hell's chance of laying nose to a trail and holding to it—more so when you wouldn't know what tracks to lay 'em to."

"You sound as if you know what you're talking about," smiled St. Andre, thinking of how accurate Calamity's description had been of what went on after the finding of other Strangler victims, and seeing why the bloodhounds failed to assist the police's search for the killer.

"Dobe and the boys are hound-running fools when they're not on the trail," Calamity explained. "They taught me some about it."

"Is there any chance of your friend following the Strangler's tracks?"

"As long as they haven't been trampled under-foot and the feller stays off the paths, ole Tophet'll follow him. I don't want you to expect Tophet to trail the Strangler to his home, but he'll point you the direction that bastard went off after killing the gal, and maybe tell you a mite more that could help."

For a moment St. Andre did not reply. As an avid student of the flood of Western fiction currently appearing in the popular press, he had read of Indians and a few white men who possessed the ability to follow a human trail by using their eyes. St. Andre had discounted the idea as being no more than another joke foisted on the stories' authors by Westerners. Knowing Calamity would not joke at such a moment, St. Andre wondered if her friend could help the police by following the Strangler's tracks.

There was one small detail to be remembered by St. Andre. The Strangler case had been assigned to Lieutenant Caiman, an older man, shrewd, tough and capable, but sadly lacking in imagination. Maybe Caiman would not care to have outsiders interfering in the investigation. Somehow St. Andre could not see Caiman taking to a newfangled notion like using a visual tracker.

"Why not bring on your tracker tonight?" he asked, deciding that what the eye did not see caused no worry to the heart of Lieutenant Caiman.

"Tophet's good," Calamity replied, "but he can't track at night, even in moonlight this good, or when he's all likkered up. Which same he's likely to be by this time. Leave it until daylight and he'll read you some sign."

"We've nothing to lose. However, it's Lieutenant Caiman's case and it will have to be his decision."

"Reckon Lou Caiman's about ready to try anything, Looten-ant," put in one of the patrolmen. "The *Intelligencer*'s been roasting his hide over the killings."

"What's that?" asked Calamity.

"A newspaper," St. Andre replied in a tone that suggested he did not care for the *New Orleans Intelligencer*. "We'll leave it to Caiman to decide. One of you stay here and don't let anybody touch the body, the other one take care of that man and the girl. Take them to the station house until Lieutenant Caiman's seen them."

Giving a distasteful grunt and a shrug, the older patrolman said he would stay on the spot and allow his partner to escort the witness to the station house. Long service had its privileges, but it also bore responsibilities. So the older man took the more unpleasant of the two assignments.

"Say, do either of you boys know her?" Calamity asked, not looking at the body again.

"It's hard to say, ma'am," the older patrolman answered. "From her clothes she worked the streets, but that covers a

38

helluva an area. From Latour Street down to the river-front you'd find hundreds like her."

"We've never managed to identify one of the victims yet, *cherie*," St. Andre went on. "The girls don't often live with their parents. In many cases only their mac would miss them. That's their—."

"I know. We call 'em the same, or say they're blacksmithing, out West," Calamity interrupted.

"No mac would come near the police, he'd merely figure his girl ran out on him and go looking for another. Let's get going, Calam, we can do no more here."

Already the younger patrolman had joined the blonde and was helping a very pale, portly man rise. Calamity looked at the blonde for a long moment, then walked towards her.

"Look, blondie," Calamity said. "Reckon you could face up to taking a peek at that gal."

An expression of shock and fear came to the blonde's face. While she had never seen one of the Strangler's victims, her instinct told her the sight must be real unpleasant.

"N—No!" she gasped. "Why should I?"

"Because that gal's the eighth to be killed. The man who killed her's got to be stopped."

"Then let the police stop him!" croaked the blonde, backing away a couple of steps and staring with horror at what she could see of the body.

"They want to," answered Calamity. "Only they've no place to start looking. Maybe if they knew who the girl was, they could make a start at finding the Strangler. Only they don't know who she is. You might."

St. Andre looked first at Calamity, then turned his eyes to the blonde. While the Strangler was not his case, the detective wanted to see it solved. Yet he knew that girls like blonde would never volunteer to help the police once clear of the crime. If she did not try to identify the body right then, the blonde would most likely be nowhere to be found the following day, unless held as a prisoner which would not make her feel in a co-operative mood on her release.

"It's possible you could help us a great deal, my pet," he said gently.

Shaking her head, the blonde tried to turn away. "I don't want to look!" she gasped, the fear of death strong on her.

"I could tell you that it's not too bad," Calamity said gently, "but I won't. That gal there looks bad." She laid her hand on the blonde's arm, stopping the other girl backing away. "It'll not be easy. Only she might be somebody you know. A pard, a kid you like."

"I don—!" began the blonde.

"Listen to me, gal," Calamity interrupted, still quietly. "The man who killed her has to be stopped. The law don't know him. Maybe if they know who the girl is they could find out who she's been with tonight, and that'll take 'em to the man who killed her."

While Calamity had no idea of how a detective worked, she figured the method she outlined might be as good a way as any of finding the Strangler. Something in Calamity's voice and touch reached the blonde, sank through her fear of what she would see and give her courage.

"I—I'll take a look."

"Good gal!" Calamity answered.

"You—You come with me," the blonde went on.

There were many things Calamity would rather have done than taking another look at that hideous body, but she kept her hand on the girl's arm and led her to the side of the corpse. The elder patrolman had covered the face with his bandana handkerchief and the sight did not look too bad. While it still retained the slightly awe-inspiring look that death always gives a human frame, the main horror stayed concealed.

"I don't know the clothes," the blonde stated, after sucking in a deep breath and looking down. "They're the sort of thing a whole heap of us girls wear."

"Try the face, Sherry," Calamity said.

Throwing a look at Calamity, St. Andre bent down. His hand touched the bandana, then he looked at the pallid-faced blonde.

"Go ahead, Sherry," Calamity ordered. "She'll take it."

With a pull, St. Andre exposed the face. He saw the blonde girl stagger and Calamity support her. For a moment St. Andre thought the blonde would faint, but a street-walker's life made her tough and hard. She mastered her emotions and looked at the face.

"N—No!" she ejaculated in a strangled voice. "I—I don't know her."

St. Andre covered the face again and came to his feet. "You're sure, my pet, that you don't know her?"

"Can't tell, the way her face is, not for sure. But I don't think I know her," answered the blonde, turning away.

"You've done well," said St. Andre. "Go with the patrolman to the station house."

Suspicion sprang to the blonde's face. "Are you arresting me?"

"No. You'll be given a cup of coffee, and sent home. See she goes by a hack and charge it to me."

"Sure, lieutenant," replied the younger patrolman. "Come on, Sally. And you, mister."

Watching the patrolman assist the portly man and blonde away, Calamity gave a shrug. "It might've worked."

"Certainly, *cherie*," replied St. Andre. "Now I must take you to your friends and then go to make my report."

"Does that feller allus jump gals?" asked Calamity as she and St. Andre walked along the path and away from the body.

"He does, if it is the same man," the detective answered. "And the same method is used, so we believe it to be the work of one man."

"I sure wish he'd try it on me," remarked Calamity, her right hand stroking the butt of her Navy Colt.

Following the direction of the girl's gesture, St. Andre remembered his duty as a policeman bound by the rules, ordinances and laws of the city.

"You'd best let me keep your gunbelt, *cherié*," he said.

"Why?"

"It's against the law to wear a gun in New Orleans—and it will give me an excuse to come and see you in the morning."

"Land-sakes, do you need an excuse for that?" grinned Calamity, but she unbuckled the gunbelt and freed the pigging thong at the bottom of the holster. "See you get it back early in the morning, mind. I want to clean the gun."

"How early is early?"

"Come as early as you like—as long as it's not too early. Say by seven, I ought to be wake by then."

"*Seven?* And you say that's not too early!"

"Sure ain't, back west of the Big Muddy. Ain't it here?"

"I mostly get into my office by nine o'clock," smiled St. Andre, not bothering to mention the numberless occasions he had worked for eighteen to fortyeight hours at a stretch without going home, when involved in a difficult case.

"Shuckens," Calamity gasped. "You city folks sure have an easy life."

Then she thought of the girl lying back on the path and decided that not all city folks had an easy life.

However, Calamity had never been one to brood on or mope about the past. Knowing there to be no chance of nailing the Strangler's hide to the wall that night she forced the memory of the dead girl from her mind and prepared to buckle down to helping her friends enjoy their first evening in New Orleans.

On leaving the Park, Calamity found herself on Latour Street, an area apparently given over almost entirely to entertainment. Saloons, a theatre, a couple of cafés, billiard halls, a dancehall and gambling houses flanked a wide street, each giving out with its own blare of noise. In many ways the street made Calamity feel at home for the first time since reaching New Orleans. This was her part of town, tough, boisterous, rowdy, like the main drag of a trail end or mining city back in the West. Maybe the buildings looked a mite more permanent, being built of brownstone instead of adobe or timber, but the noises and sights reminded Calamity of the kind of places she knew and loved.

A couple of bouncers heaved a drunk from one saloon, sending him flying across the pavement to narrowly miss landing in one of the large horse-troughs that lined the street. Calamity ignored the drunk and studied the water-filled troughs.

"You sure have some thirsty hosses down here," she remarked.

"Not really," St. Andre answered. "We use them in case of fire. There's the *Cheval D'Or* now."

Coming to a halt before the largest, noisiest and most garish place on the street, Calamity looked it over with critical gaze. "Sure looks fancy. Say, are you coming in for a drink?"

"I have work to do, *cherie*," the detective replied, taking her hand in his, carrying to it his lips and kissing it.

"First time anybody ever kissed my *hand*," Calamity stated. "I sure hope that ain't the only place you fellers kiss."

"That," St. Andre told her with a grin. "Is something you will have to wait to discover. *Au revoir, cherie.*"

"I don't know what it means," replied Calamity, "but the same to you, and many of them."

With that Miss Martha Jane Canary turned and entered the *Cheval D'Or*.

# CHAPTER FIVE

*Miss Canary At The Cheval D'Or.*

DESPITE its fancy-sounding name, the bar-room of the *Cheval D'Or* appeared to be little or no different from the kind of place Calamity had looked upon in a whole heap of top-grade saloons throughout the West—with one exception. A small but rowdy band played music at the left side of the room and instead of performing on the stage, the saloon's show girls whirled and kicked their legs in the centre of the open space mostly left free for public dancing. The crowd lining the long bar, or seated at the various tables, lacked cowhands, buckskin-clad plainsmen, yet seemed to be little different from a Western saloon's customers in class or social standing; except for the folk at a couple of the tables on a small raised section close to the band. From the expensive clothing of the people on the dais, the fact that a couple of waiters showered attention on them full-time, and that champagne appeared to be the popular tipple served, Calamity figured them to belong to the richer class, the women of the party included.

Out West the 'good' women only very rarely entered a saloon, and ladies of the upper classes more than most stayed out of the places of entertainment. However, in New Orleans, and other Eastern cities, the desire to see how the other half relaxed and played became fashionable and brought parties of socialites to better class saloons to do so. Or course the socialites did not wish for too close contact with the revelling *hoi polloi*, so the obliging saloon-owners—always eager to satisfy the whims of well-paying customers—erected little segregated areas, often with their own private entrances, on which those who had the right background, and could afford it, might sit in comfort and see the fun. From their little raised sanctums, the ladies looked down on the herd enjoying its pleasures, watched shows which they regarded as being thrillingly naughty, and left with a sense of having improved their knowledge of life.

After a tolerant glance at the champagne-sipping upper-crust, Calamity forgot them and scanned the room for her friends. Sure enough the boys sat right where she figured they would be, at a table slap-bang on the edge of the dance floor and from where they could have an uninterrupted view of all that went on. Big, burly, white-haired Dobe Killem, her boss; lean, dark and tough looking Tophet Tombes, who acted as scout for the outfit; Chan Sing, the Chinese cook whose lapse from grace first gave Calamity acceptance to the outfit, and the other boys sat at ease, or as near at ease as their shop-bought, city-style clothes allowed, drinking whisky, squiring half-a-dozen or so saloongirls and ogling the waving black-stockings and exposed white thighs of the dancers.

Calamity gave the dancing girls a casual glance as she walked across the room to join her friends. With one exception, the girls dancing looked nor performed no better than she had seen in Western saloons. Mind you, that exception danced a heap more fancy than Calamity could ever remember seeing anywhere. The exception was a girl Calamity's size, with a slim, but shapely figure in an abbreviated white outfit that left her arms and legs bare and who wore—although Calamity did not know them as such—ballet slippers on her feet. Showing far greater grace, agility and style, the girl whirled, spun and kicked her well-muscled legs in a manner that made the others look heavy-footed as a bunch of miners at a hoe-down. Her red hair was taken back and pinned up at the rear in a severe fashion, and her rather pale but pretty face held an expression of rapture as if she enjoyed every minute of her dance.

A man, engrossed in watching the red-haired dancer's gyrations on the points of her ballet slippers, felt Calamity bump into him as she crossed the room, glanced at her, turned back to observe the dancer, then swivelled his head hurriedly to Calamity's departing figure. For a moment he stared after Calamity and rubbed his eyes. Deciding that he had better stop drinking, for he could not possibly have just seen a pretty girl dressed in men's clothes pass him—although, if it came to a point, the feller who bumped into him sure walked fancy —the man emptied his glass and left the room.

"Hey, Calam gal!" whooped Dobe Killem, eyeing his protege. "Come and get sat down, gal. Damn it, where've you been to?"

Suspicion gleamed in the saloon-girls' eyes as Calamity took the offered seat. Unlike the man Calamity bumped into, they knew for certain the newcomer was a woman and did not care for the idea of an outsider moving in on what showed signs of developing into a real humdinger of a party.

"They're my brothers, all of 'em," Calamity remarked, reading the signs as if the other girls bore them painted on their bosoms.

44

She reached for the drink Killem poured and went on in explanation. "My mother had a fast hoss."

Then she grinned at the men of the outfit, wondering if any of them would have dared walk into a Western saloon dressed in those derby hats, white shirts, fancy neck-ties and town suits. Dared might not be the correct word, for those freight-hauling sons feared nothing but their boss.

"Where've you been to, Calam gal?" asked Tophet Tombes, who looked about as at home in his new clothes as a skunk would in a church hall. "We waited, but you didn't show."

"I got lost," admitted Calamity. "Then I ran into a young feller as needed some help from four jaspers who was walking all over his face."

"Trust you!" said Killem dryly. "There's time I reckon we should ought to call you 'Trouble', not Calamity,"

"Calamity!" giggled one of the girls. "That's a funny name."

"Likely," answered Calamity, eyeing the girl with a warning stare. "Only don't push it, sister, or you'll wind up with a set of ingrowing buck-teeth."

Anger glowed in the other girl's eyes as she glanced towards her friends for moral and actual support. Slapping a big hand on the table top, Killem glared around at the girls, his bland face filled with innocent-featured malevolence.

"Now hold it there, all of you!" he ordered. "Just listen good to me, 'cause I don't aim to say it twice. Calam here's part of my outfit. You mean-mouth her and she'll whup the whole boiling of you, which same'll spoil all our evenings. So you be nice and friendly with her. You hear me?"

Within certain bounds the girls were taught to regard the customer as always being right. So far they had been treated royally by the free-spending freighters and did not wish to slaughter a goose which laid such frequent golden eggs. Several of their fellow workers eyed the party with calculating gaze and would not hesitate to move in should any of the men give a hint of displeasure. Anyway, that girl in pants did not look as if she aimed to give them any competition.

Although quite willing to take on the saloon-girls individually or as a bunch, Calamity felt no desire to spoil her friends' evening so early on. Catching the attention of a passing waiter, she ordered drinks for the table and it was taken as a peace-offering by the other girls.

After a few more leg kicks, the dancers came to a halt in a bent forward posture that flipped up their skirts, exposed frilly-edged, short-legged panties to view and caused Killem to make a hurried grab which hauled one of the over-stimulated freighters back into his seat. With a bound, the red-haired solo performer sailed into the air and landed on the floor in a split which brought a gasp from Calamity. However, the girl bounced to her feet without any sign of injury, dropped a graceful curtsy in reply to the applause which rose high, and skipped off the dancing space, between the tables and out through a door at the side of the bar.

"Where at's the gambling?" asked Calamity as the applause died down.

"Upstairs," answered one of the girls, hoping Calamity would go, for she did not feel entirely happy at having the red-head at the table.

"Hah!" grunted Tombes. "You don't want no gambling, Calam gal. It air plumb sinful—and awful chancy too."

Listening to Tombes' sombre tones, Calamity might have taken the warning seriously had she not known him so well. On the way down river a well-dressed stranger inveigled Tombes and Killem into a game of poker. While neither gave any sign of their wisdom, both possessed a very thorough knowledge of all branches of the gambling business. On the fourth deal Killem objected to the dealer extracting for the improvement of a hand the seven of clubs from the bottom of the deck. Killem was 'dressed' at the time, and possessed a fair amount of skill in the speedy production of a weapon—leaning to his sheathed bowie knife on that occasion—and so was in a good position to make his point. A series of gambling scandals had recently rocked the Mississippi, causing the riverboat captains to be less tolerant of crooked gamblers than had formerly been the case. So the errant well-dressed stranger found himself penniless and standing on a sand bar, leaving Killem's outfit to share out eighteen hundred dollars of his money. In addition to their pay from a freighting trip to Fort Sherrard in the Dakota Territory, an advance of wages and expense money donated by the Army, the gambler's contribution ensured that the Killem bunch were well fixed to enjoy their visit to New Orleans.

Calamity decided to forego her investigation of the *Cheval D'Or's* games of chance and sat back in her chair to see how the saloon compared with a Western place in the matter of entertainment. After a brief rest, the band struck up with a lively tune and the saloon-girls led most of the men out on to the open space. Never one for dancing, except when toting more 'Old Whipping

46

Post' whisky than at present, Tombes remained at the table with Calamity. Taking her opportunity, Calamity told the leathery-faced scout of the incident in the Park, also about the suggestion she made utilising his knowledge of the ancient and honourable art of reading sign Western style.

"We'll take us a look whether he likes it or not, comes morning," Tombes stated when Calamity remarked that the final decision must come from one Lieutenant Caiman who she had not yet met. "Damn it, gal, I'd sure like to lay hands on that there Strangler."

"And me," Calamity answered, then her eyes swung from Tombes to gaze across the room with all the intent eagerness of a starving Cheyenne seeing a herd of prime Great Plains buffalo. "Say, who's that big gal there?"

Following the direction of Calamity's gaze and jerked thumb, Tombes studied the woman who so aroused his companion's interest. Big was no exaggeration when describing the woman. She stood nearly six foot tall and weighed at least two hundred pounds. Blonde hair piled high on the woman's head and her fat, jovial face carried stage make-up. Expensive-looking jewellery glinted around her neck, wrists and fingers and she wore a trailing, stylish, though tight-fitting blue dress.

"That's Madam Darcel, gal, the owner," Tombes explained and gave a warning for he knew Calamity. "And you forget it. She'd call the great siezer in and have you jailed happen you tried to start a brawl with her."

A grin creased Calamity's face at Tombes' insight of her character. "She'd be a mite too heavy anyways."

"Likely," the scout replied. "Just look at ole Dobe dance."

"He's about as graceful as a salmon-fed grizzly just afore winter," the girl answered. "Happen that black-haired gal ain't lively on her feet, she'll sure wind up with tired toes comes the end of the dance."

Although Killem's partner limped slightly as she returned to the table, her face held a smile. A saloon-girl learned to look happy under most conditions, even after having her toes stepped on by a partner who stood six foot two and carried a fair amount of weight. A round of drinks, bought this time by Chan Sing, who had a plump, dark-haired girl hanging to his arm, made Killem's partner feel happier.

For a time the party went on, drinks flowed, jokes bounced around the table and most of the girls appeared to be overlooking Calamity's sex, regarding her more as a paying customer rather than a rival.

Turning to the girl at her side, Calamity asked, "Hey, where'd a gal go, happen she wants to go?"

"Huh?" asked the puzzled saloon-girl, then the light glowed. "Oh! I'll show you where we go."

Watching Calamity and the saloon-girl walk away from the table, Killem thought over what Calamity had told him about her rescue of St. Andre. A grin came to the big freighter's face. Dang that Calamity, never happy unless she was mixed up in some fuss or ruckus; but life would sure be dull without her around.

The dark-haired girl seated on Chan Sing's knee had only recently come to work at the *Cheval D'Or* after being employed in a rather lower-class establishment further along Latour Street. In her previous post, the management expected her to augment her salary by collecting donations from the customers—without their being aware, of the removal of their wealth—and reckoned the same rule applied at the *Cheval D'Or*. Deciding the Chinaman would offer her the best possibilities, she latched on to him and had been on the point of extracting his wallet when Calamity arrived. Since then, the girl had not found an opportunity to take the wallet, for Calamity had none of the distractions offered to her male friends. Naturally when augmenting her salary without the owner of the wallet's permission, one required privacy. So the girl left Chang Sing's wallet where it rightfully belonged. When Calamity left, the girl thought she might find a chance. Seconds ticked by with nothing to take the attention of the other occupants of the table. Then a couple of jugglers made their appearance and the men gave the performers their attention.

Still keeping one arm around Sing's neck, the girl slipped her other hand into his jacket and slid out the wallet. Being skilled at her trade, Sing did not feel his loss and the girl believed her action went unnoticed. So it did among the occupants of the table—however, somebody had seen the move, a person well capable of dealing with the matter.

The dark-haired girl's first warning that things had gone wrong came as she prepared to slip the wallet into the front of her dress. Suddenly a strong hand dug fingers deep into her hair, twisted hard, and hauled her from Sing's knee.

With a screech of pain, the girl twisted around, though still held by the hair, and faced her assailant. The wallet fell from the girl's fingers as she prepared to defend herself against Calamity who, having seen the attempted theft, came to the rescue of her unsuspecting friend. Before the girl could make a hostile move, Calamity swung her hand in a slap which caught the other across the cheek. Showing superb timing, Calamity released the girl's hair and the force of the slap sent the pickpocket staggering backwards. After taking several steps to the rear, the girl tripped and landed hard, rump-first on the floor at the centre of the open area.

Spitting curses, the girl started to rise. She was slightly taller and heavier than Calamity and noted for being a tough dame when riled, which same she appeared to be at the moment. An air of eager anticipation ran through the room. On the upper-class dais all chatter stopped and every eye turned to the dance floor. Predatory interest crept on to the men's faces—although the upper-crust males were not alone in that—and the women pretended to be shocked at the sight, while waiting eagerly to see the next drama of raw, lower-strata life being played before them.

Even as the dark-haired girl prepared to throw herself at Calamity and take revenge for the slap, a deep voice boomed out a warning.

"All right, my children! Enough of this folly."

Calamity took her eyes from the other girl for long enough to glance quickly at the speaker. From the authoritative tones, she could have guessed it to be the mountainous Madam Darcel who spoke. The big woman bore down on the girls like a battleship in full sail. While in the girl's toilet Calamity had removed her jacket and carried it back. The tight fitting shirt and levis left no doubt as to her sex. She did not relax, but kept her attention on the other girl after her quick glance in Madam Darcel's direction.

Instead of throwing herself at Calamity, the dark-haired girl prepared to bluff her way out. Still crouched ready to spring, the girl turned a sullen, defiant face, that bore just a hint of fear, to her employer.

"What is all this about?" Madam Darcel went on.

"That dame grabbed me—!" began the saloon-girl.

"Sure I did," agreed Calamity and pointed to the wallet lying on the floor. "Do you let your gals lift wallets from the customers?"

Throwing a scared glance at the big shape of Madam Darcel, the saloon-girl gave a screech of, "It's a lie!" and threw herself at Calamity, hoping the ensuing fracas might silence the red-head and evade the issue of whether she stole the wallet. Only she did not reach Calamity with her talon-like, grabbing hands.

With a surge of her shoulder, Madam Darcel propelled her big right fist forward so it crashed on to the saloon-girl's jaw. The force of the blow sent the girl shooting off course even before Calamity could take steps to meet the attack and the pickpocket landed on the dance floor, sliding almost to the bar before coming to a stop in a limp heap.

Calamity studied the blow with the air of a connoisseur. While it looked just a touch slow, that right hand packed such weight and power behind it that on landing would cause the recipient to think the roof had fallen in on her—when she found herself capable of thinking again, that is.

Glancing at Chan Sing as the Chinaman stood feeling in his jacket's breast pocket, Madam Darcel knew she must prove that she had no knowledge of the theft and did not condone stealing. Nothing could lose the carriage-trade for a saloon quicker than letting thieves rob the customers, or by the place gaining a reputation for dishonesty. The feeling of the girl had been the first stage, now Madam Darcel aimed to cement the knowledge of her innocence more firmly in the minds of her customers.

"Is that your wallet, John?" she asked, pointing to the floor.

"By clacky, it is!" Sing yelped, bending and picking the wallet up.

"I don't allow pickpockets in here," the saloonkeeper went on in a loud and carrying voice, then looked towards the silent bar. "Eddy, see this gent gets anything he orders for the rest of the evening, on the house."

"Sure will, Madam," answered the head bartender, catching his cue and following it up like a professional actor.

A low rumble of approval ran through the room which had fallen silent and expectant at the start of the trouble. Madam Darcel knew her actions had cleared her and figured the money it would cost to keep the Chinaman supplied for the rest of the evening to be a cheap price when her house's reputation had been at stake.

Then Madam turned her attention to Calamity. The saloon-keeper's first thought was that Calamity followed the profession of street-walker and dressed in men's clothing to gain entrance to the *Cheval D'Or* in search of customers. On studying the girl more closely, Madam Darcel revised her opinion. No street-walker, working at night and following an unhealthy trade, ever carried such a tan as did the red head. Possibly the girl was a camp-follower of the Killem outfit, brought down to New Orleans to save hiring local talent. Whoever the red-head might be, Madam Darcel did not intend to let her stay in the saloon.

"All right, girlie," the saloonkeeper said. I don't like trouble-makers in here—."

"So who's making trouble?" Calamity replied. "I've got good

money in my pocket, I'm sober, white and old enough to do a hard day's work—and I'm staying right here."

Madam Darcel read the challenge in Calamity's eyes and an idea crept into the saloonkeeper's head, showing her a chance of some added entertainment to spice up her customers. With a clientele that liked its fun gamey, unrefined and fullblooded, a fight between two girls had a salutary effect on the spirits and also the sales over the bar. Unless Madam missed her guess, that red-headed girl could handle her end in such an affair. So there only remained the problem of selecting a suitable opponent and that was easily arranged.

Not that Madam Darcel intended to be the one who took on Calamity. The days had long passed when the saloon-keeper could trim down a tough young girl who knew the art of female self defence. While Madam did not doubt that she could lay Calamity low with one blow, there remained the problem of making contact with her fist. From the look of her, the red-head would not be fool enough to stand still to be hit, nor unprepared as the pickpocket had been.

"Are you going quietly?" Madam asked.

Throwing back her head and standing with hands on her hips, but ready to dodge a blow and attack, Calamity roared with laughter and replied, "I never go anyplace quietly."

"And what if I have you thrown out?" said the saloon-keeper.

"Are you fixing to do it yourself?" Calamity countered.

"Not I. But one of my girls will."

"Happen you got a gal who reckons she can do it, bring her on and let her get to throwing."

In her untrained way Calamity was every bit as much a show-man as Madam Darcel. Both spoke loudly and their words carried around the silent room. Calamity glanced around her, studying the girls. While some of them looked hefty, rough and capable, none struck Calamity as being anything special. Anyways, it ought to be right interesting to see how a big-city girl stacked up in comparison with some of the tough dames Calamity tangled with out West.

Madam Darcel hid her delight as Calamity accepted the challenge. Turning, the saloonkeeper called, "Hey one of you, ask Jacqueline to come in here."

Grinning broadly, Calamity walked towards her friends' table and wondered who Jacqueline might be.

# CHAPTER SIX

*Miss Canary Studies Savate*

"Good ole Calam!" Tophet said as he listened to the girl accept Madam Darcel's challenge. "Trust her to fix it so to we could win us some money."

"She'll take that city gal like Grant took Richmond," another of the outfit went on, remembering other times when Calamity tied into a saloongirl in a brawl.

Despite his men's words of confidence, Killem did not feel so sure. Not that he lacked faith in Calamity, but he knew Madam Darcel of old. If Madam aimed to start a brawl between Calamity and one of the saloon's girls, the big woman figured to have a better than fair chance of her representative winning.

"Hold hard there, Madam," he called. "Reckon you don't know who my gal is."

"I don't care if she is Calamity Jane—," Madam began.

"That's just who she is."

Talk welled up at Killem's words, eager and excited chatter, for the name of Calamity Jane had come down river ahead of her. Yet few of the occupants of the room really believed the girl to be *the* Calamity Jane. Certainly Madam Darcel did not believe Killem and thought the freighter merely wanted to save his girl from a thrashing. Madam did not intend to state her doubts. One glance around—taken with her considerable knowledge of human nature—told her the crowd wanted the red-head to be Calamity Jane; much as hold-up victims always wanted to believe some famous outlaw band robbed them. So Madam went along with the suggestion as if she took Killem to be speaking the gospel truth.

"I have heard of her, Dobe. But I also believe Jacqueline can throw even the famous Calamity Jane out."

"I've got fifty dollars that says she can't!" whooped Tombes.

"You-all wanting to bet your gal can do it, Madam?" went on another man.

"If you wish," Madam replied.

"We wish!" whooped the freighters. "Lordy lord, how we wish."

With that the Killem outfit produced its money and Madam signalled one of her men to accept the wagers. Apart from the freighters, there was little betting so far, the other customers wanting to compare the fighters before risking wealth on one or the other.

Calamity ignored the betting as she walked to Killem's table. The girl who had escorted Calamity to the toilets handed back the jacket she took on observing the attempted theft of Sing's wallet.

"Thanks, Maisie," grinned Calamity. "Say, who is this Jacqueline."

"You've seen her once tonight," replied the girl.

While waiting for the mysterious Jacqueline to put in an appearance, Calamity prepared for the fight. Taking off her kepi, she laid it on her jacket. Next she removed her bandana, rolling it into a ball and dropping it into the crown of her kepi. Calamity always removed her bandana, given time to do so, since a girl almost choked her insensible in an early fight by grabbing hold and twisting at the neck cloth.

"What's eating you, Dobe?" she asked, glancing at Killem's face and reading his concern where most folks could have seen nothing at all.

"Was just wondering what sort of gal Madam's got in mind," the freighter answered. "Maybe this Jacqueline's one of them gal prize-fighters like was with that wagon train that went to Fort Sherrard with us last trip."

"Shucks," grinned Calamity. "I whipped that one, and she claimed to be the champeen gal fist-fighter of the world. Don't reckon this Jacqueline gal'll be any tougher'n that one." *

"Here she comes now," said one of the saloon-girls, pointing across the room.

Turning from the table, Calamity glanced in the direction indicated by the other girl. Killem and his men also looked and the big freighter felt puzzled by what he saw. However, Killem's men, possibly because they did not share his ability to carry a load of liquor, nudged each other and exchanged knowing nods or winks. The men, with the exception of Killem, agreed that if the girl who approached was *the* Jacqueline, Calamity should lick her so easy that the bets would be as safe as finding money in the street.

For a moment Calamity studied her proposed opponent, then swung to face Madam Darcel, wondering if the other woman made a joke.

*Told in TROUBLE TRAIL by J. T. Edson. Wagon Wheel Western.

"Is this *her?*" asked Calamity.

"It is."

"Hell, you can't expect her to tangle with me."

"Why should she not?" inquired Madam Darcel.

"That skinny kid won't have a chance," replied Calamity.

Yet she was no fool and, like Killem, knew that Madam Darcel would be most unlikely to act as a philanthropist by taking bets when, on the face of it, the saloon's representative had no hope of winning. With that thought in mind Calamity had been expecting to find herself matched by a big, buxom, tough girl. Instead she found herself faced by the slim, red-headed girl who performed as a solo dancer. The red-head still wore the same outfit as when dancing, including her ballet slippers—a point Calamity overlooked.

Annoyance glowed in Jacqueline's eyes at Calamity's words. In an age when the ideal female tended to be buxom, Jacqueline was conscious of her slim though shapely build and did not care for Calamity's reference to her as 'that skinny kid'.

"Are you afraid?" hissed Jacqueline.

"I sure am," agreed Calamity. "Afraid I'll hurt you real bad."

"Let *me* worry about that!"

Frowning a little, Calamity gave the other girl a close study. One thing was for sure, that scanty costume prevented any chance of Jacqueline being a young man dressed as a girl, a possibility that had occured to Calamity. Nor did it allow Jacqueline to carry concealed weapons; not that Calamity figured Madam would chance such a thing. While slim, Jacqueline's hips were well developed, her long legs showed a good set of thigh and calf muscles. Yet she did not have the weight to take on a girl Calamity's build. Calamity enjoyed a fight, but she had never been a bully or wished to take an unfair advantage of anybody.

"Hell, Madam!" Calamity objected. "This's not fair on your gal."

"She seems content to take her chances," Madam answered. "I'll tell you what I'll do. I'll give the winner five dollars for every minute the fight lasts."

Calamity shrugged, the financial side of the affair meant little or nothing to her. Having leaned over backwards to save Jacqueline from a licking, Calamity reckoned she had done enough. However, even with the prospect of earning five dollars for every minute she kept the other girl standing, Calamity decided to make a rapid end to the affair. Once she sent Jacqueline tearfully on her way, Calamity reckoned she would see how tough Madam Darcel could act and teach the big blonde not to send her employees to take a licking when they did not have a chance.

"It's her that gets the lumps," Calamity remarked.

"Start as soon as you like," replied Madam Darcel and went to join Killem.

Calamity threw a glance at the slim girl, then grinned at Dobe Killem.

"This won't take long, Dobe," she said. "I'll be right back."

And Calamity spoke truer words than she imagined.

With fists clenched ready, she moved towards the Creole girl and wondered how the other aimed to make her fight. Calamity found out soon enough. Watching Jacqueline's eyes and hands, Calamity overlooked the other girl's feet. Suddenly and without any warning Jacqueline kicked upwards her long right leg driving into the air to catch Calamity under the jaw. Taken by surprise both by the unexpected tactic and the power of the kick, Calamity sprawled backwards and landed on her rump at Killem's feet.

"That fat old bitch!" Killem growled, looking at the smiling saloonkeeper. "She's thrown Calam against a *savate* fighter."

Calamity did not hear the words. Forcing herself to her feet, she charged into the attack once more. Much to Calamity's surprise, Jacqueline moved forward to meet her as if ready for a hair-yanking tangle. Only at the last moment the slim girl side-stepped, leaned out of Calamity's reach and delivered a horizontal sidekick, her toe catching Calamity in the stomach. Giving a croaking gasp, Calamity grabbed at her middle and doubled over as she staggered by Jacqueline. Pivoting gracefully, the slim girl placed her foot against Calamity's tight-stretched pants seat and shoved hard. Calamity shot forward to crash into the bar. Grabbing hold of the polished mahogany, she hung there while she tried to catch her wind and clear the fog from her head.

Just as Calamity regained control of herself and turned, Jacqueline came gliding in. Halting before Calamity, the dancer rose on to the point of her right slipper and executed an almost perfect *fouette en tournant* by whipping her raised left leg from bent at the knee to extended waist high so as to spin her entire body around. Four times she spun in a circle, gaining momentum. Then the toe of her left foot crashed into the side of Calamity's jaw. The impact sprawled Calamity sideways even as she prepared to make an attack of her own.

While Jacqueline did not particularly care for fighting, she meant to keep the brawl going for a time. Nor did Calamity's insulting references to the dancer's slim build entirely account for the decision.

Ever since the day Jacqueline sneaked into a theatre and saw a ballet dancer perform, she longed to learn the secrets of the graceful art. Being from a very poor family, she had no chance of taking formal lessons. She took every opportunity to see other dancers and practiced the steps she saw, learning the various positions and manoeuvres even without knowing their names. Two years back Madam Darcel had seen the girl dancing on a street corner and recognised her talent, so hired Jacqueline to perform at the *Cheval D'Or*. From then Jacqueline improved tremendously, yet lacked formal instruction to bring out her talented greatness.

Learning *savate* came as a precaution against the petty jealousies of the saloongirls and Jacqueline found it a useful way of augmenting her earnings. On the dozen or so occasions when she fought another before the customers, Madam Darcel gave her a bonus and when the money went to swell her slowly-growing savings ready for the day when she could afford to take lessons at a ballet school.

So while another kick might have finished Calamity off, the slim girl did not land it. Instead she slapped Calamity's face with each hand, rocking the red-head from side to side. Pain partially cleared Calamity's spinning head and she thrust herself from the bar, throwing a punch which ought to have flattened her at Jacqueline's head. The blow missed as Jacqueline whirled aside and Calamity stumbled forward. Twisting around, Jacqueline delivered a slap to Calamity's rump as the red-head went by.

Then began the most humiliating five minutes of Calamity's life. Laughter and jeers rang out from the watching crowd as Calamity tried to catch up with, or lay hands on the other girl. Gracefully, and demonstrating her dancing skill to perfection, Jacqueline avoided Calamity's rushes and wild blows. Sometimes she would whirl around Calamity so fast that the other girl did not know whether she came or went, then stop in front and slap her face, or halt behind and either push her, deliver a whack to her rump or push her. No matter which way Calamity turned, she could not catch the other girl. It seemed that Jacqueline could deliver a kick from any angle, and when one landed, whether with toe, ball, heel, outside or inside edge of the foot, it hurt.

Blood trickled from Calamity's mouth, mingling with the sweat and tears on her face. Pain, rage and humiliation filled the Western girl at the thought of taking such a licking from a city dweller. It forced Calamity to stay up and take more of those wicked horizontal and vertical kicks while trying to lay hands on Jacqueline and fight barroom style.

Only once did Calamity try to take Jacqueline by the slim girl's own method of fighting. Jerking back her leg, Calamity launched it in a kick. Jacqueline watched the other girl's right foot lash at her legs and countered the kick by coming into the *chasse croise* position so Calamity missed her. Then as Calamity's leg went by, Jacqueline brought the side of her right foot in a circular kick against the Western girl's calf. Caught off balance, Calamity staggered and Jacqueline followed up with a kick to the pants seat which sprawled her on to the floor. Skipping forward Jacqueline gripped Calamity by the hair and waist belt, hauling her up. Before Calamity recovered enough to defend herself, Jacqueline delivered a high kick to her face and started her nose bleeding.

"Damn it hell, Madam!" Killem growled, watching Jacqueline spin away from Calamity. "She's making a fool of my gal."

"I thought your girl feared hurting Jacqueline," replied the saloonkeeper. "If your friends are willing to concede their bets, I will signal Jacqueline to make an end of this farce."

"You'd best do that afore these boys of mine get riled and take your place apart at the seams."

Before Madam could decide whether to make the signal, Jacqueline prepared to bring the affair to an end. Never had she seen a girl take so much punishment. On other occasions, her opponent took at the most half-a-dozen kicks then either collapsed and refused to rise, or ran sobbing from the room. Yet the Western girl kept coming back for more, trying to lay hands on her tormentor. Jacqueline guessed that even now it would go rough on her if Calamity did once get to grips. So she decided to make an end to the affair. The kick to the face had sent Calamity stumbling into the bar where she hung on for support, her legs looking like heat-buckled candles. From her opponent's general appearance, Jacqueline decided that honour had been satisfied and it would be a long time before the red-headed Westerner insulted another slimly-built girl.

Once more Jacqueline went into her *fouette en tournant*, building up her momentum to deliver a *coup de grace*. In this she made a bad error in judgement. No other girl Jacqueline had tangled with, even those trained in *savate*—after seeing the interest Jacqueline attracted for the *Cheval D'Or*, other saloonkeepers sought out challengers to meet her—faced her with such determination. So Jacqueline reckoned that one more kick ought to stretch Calamity out on the floor, limp and unable to prevent the slim girl gripping her by the feet and hauling her from the room. Once outside, Madam's bouncers would take over, carrying the beaten Western girl to the rear of the saloon, call in a doctor if needed, and revive her. Then Madam Darcel would most likely give the beaten girl a few dollars to recompense her.

Jacqueline's thoughts came to an abrupt and painful end right then. Even as the slim girl spun around on her right slipper's point, Calamity forced herself from the bar and swung a fist around in a looping blow. Taken by surprise, unable to stop her spinning body, Jacqueline swung straight into the punch which stopped her dead in her tracks. Like a flash Calamity struck again, ripping her other hand up as Killem taught her, catching Jacqueline under the jaw and sending her reeling backwards to crash on to the floor.

Turning to the bar, Calamity caught its top and steadied herself, looking at the bartender. "Gi—Gimme—a—drink!" she gasped.

Obligingly the man poured out four fingers of whisky and passed the glass to Calamity. Tilting the liquor down her throat in a single gulp, Calamity glanced into the bar mirror. Much to her surprise, Calamity saw the other girl struggling to rise. Setting down her glass, Calamity turned and crossed the floor. She bent down and dug her fingers into Jacqueline's hair, ruining its coiffure for the first time in the fight. With a heave Calamity raised the other girl to her feet, swung her and sent her reeling across the room into the bar.

At that moment Jacqueline forgot *savate*. Dazed and hurt by the blows, the slim girl became a woman pure and simple. Suddenly she thrust herself from the bar and met Calamity's advance, her fingers digging into the other's red curls. Calamity replied in a like manner and the girls spun around in a tight circle, clinging to hair, lashing out wild kicks at each other's legs and forgetting more scientific fighting. More by accident than design, Jacqueline hooked a leg behind Calamity and brought them both crashing to the floor.

Despite her earlier rough handling, Calamity buckled down to a real old-fashioned, roll-around, hand-scalping bar-room brawl with all her usual gusto. Nor did Jacqueline fail to do her share. Out-weighed by Calamity, not as strong as the Western girl, Jacqueline's wiry body had strength to spare and she gave almost as good as she took. Over and over the girls rolled, fists and legs flying, gasps, squeaks, squeals and yelps rising from them.

During the earlier stages of the fight, the crowd, though rowdy, stayed either seated or standing well clear and watched the girls. However, once Calamity and Jacqueline went to the floor, those of the audience at the rear found they could no longer see the sport. So they moved forward and in doing so impeded the view of other customers, causing those impeded to also leave their seats until the dance floor and fighting girls were surrounded by an almost solid wall of wildly excited, yelling people.

At that point of the proceedings, Madame Darcel began to feel like the man who caught a tiger by the tail and could not let go. Without ever having heard of or understanding the words, Madam Darcel possessed a very thorough knowledge of crowd psychology; and knew that when excitement reached a certain pitch any slight thing might start a full-scale riot. Yet she knew that if she attempted to separate the wildly fighting girls, the crowd would object violently; not only because their fun was being spoiled, but because quite a number of the customers had bet heavily on the result of the fight. So she stayed out of the affair, leaving the girls to settle their dispute and keeping a weather eye open for potential spreaders of the conflict.

Coming to their feet, the girls stood facing each other, panting and glaring.

"H—Had enough?" asked Calamity.

Jacqueline did not answer in words. Instead she flung herself at Calamity again. Normally she would have used *savate*, just as Calamity's self defence ought to have been with her fists, but exhaustion caused the girls to forget such tactics and fight on woman-style. Reeling across the room, clinging one-handed to hair, the other slapping, punching and grabbing, the girls caused a hurried scattering among the crowd, all of whom knew better than come between a pair of furiously fighting females. Still locked with each other, the girls hit against the upper-classes dais. Pinned against the raised stand, Calamity wriggled back upon it. Jacqueline followed her under the protective rail and the girls came to their feet. One of the waiters, outraged at the invasion of the carriage-trade's privacy, moved forward to either request or force the girls to leave. In this the man showed mighty poor judgement and sense. Coming between a pair of bobcats scrapping over a mate would have been on a par with getting between Calamity and Jacqueline at such a moment. The girls turned on the waiter—a man chosen more for his knowledge of upper-class requirements than those qualities necessary when dealing with the rougher elements of the saloon's clientele—and worked him over. To the accompaniment of yells and laughter from the onlookers, fingers tore at the waiter's hair and clothes, feet hacked at his shins and a set of teeth at one point clamped on his ear, giving him a painful nip. Then the girls shoved the waiter aside and sent him sprawling over the protective railing into the crowd beyond.

Having dealt with the interruption, Calamity and Jacqueline turned their attention to each other. The occupants of the dais, three men and two young women at one table and a couple of young bloods squiring a beautiful girl at another, all came to their feet and looked on. None of them knew if the fight be merely something arranged by Madam Darcel for their entertainment, or cared. All showed the same excited stimulation as did the *hoi polloi* beyond the barrier at the wild fight they were seeing.

A shove from Jacqueline sent Calamity reeling to fall on the table of the larger party. One of the women, a beautiful, if rather sullen-looking blonde in an expensive satin dress, did something she thought to be wildly amusing. Stepping forward, she took an open champagne bottle from its ice bucket and emptied its contents over Calamity's head, shrieking with laughter as the fizzing liquid ran over the red-head's face.

Across the room Dobe Killem watched and gave a groan, for he knew his Calamity very well. That upper-crust girl was due very shortly to learn the error of her ways, or Killem would be most surprised.

# CHAPTER SEVEN

*Miss Canary's Soothing Syrup*

WHILE Calamity had tasted champagne on a couple of occasions, and decided that as a drink it would never replace whisky, she objected to having it poured over her head even as a joke. Although she felt no resentment or antipathy towards folks more fortunate than herself in the possession of the world's goods, Calamity failed to subscribe to Madam Darcel's view that the upper-class customers must be treated as sacred and permitted to take liberties.

Shooting out a hand as she forced herself from the table, Calamity caught the blonde in the same manner that she grabbed the pickpocket earlier. With a heave, Calamity plucked the blonde from the bosom of her friends and jerked her forward. Letting out a startled squeal, the blonde dropped the champagne bottle as Calamity swung her around and gave her a push which sent her staggering. Striking the protective rail, the blonde's weight broke it and she fell into the arms of the laughing, jeering crowd. Set on her feet, the blonde swung around. A female face came before the blonde, so wild with rage and mortification, she swung a resounding slap at it. Already over-excited by the fight she had seen, the blonde's victim forgot that the carriage-trade was to be treated as sacrosant, and grabbed hair. With a screech of pain, the blonde dropped lady-like dignity and a second hand-scalping battle began. Not a bad one either, considering that blonde's upbringing and education sadly lacked in such matters.

On the dais, the blonde's female friend gave a yell as she saw the assault. Excitement and stimulation at watching the pagan sight of two girls fighting led the second into folly. Grabbing up a bottle by its neck, the girl, a brunette of some charm and attraction, started around the table, meaning to attack Calamity and avenge her friend.

Also moving in to the attack, Jacqueline caught a movement from the corner of her eye. Turning her head to check more thoroughly on what attracted her attention, she saw the bottle-armed brunette approaching. The sight recalled Jacqueline's *savate* training once more. Like a flash Jacqueline rotated her body half a turn to the left, leant forward from the waist, drew up her right leg under her, pointed its toe at the charging brunette and kicked upwards. She caught the brunette under the jaw with the bottom of her foot, landing an almost classic *savate* horizontal high-kick. The force of the impact shot the brunette to one side. Dropping the bottle, she staggered full into the female member of the other party. The two girls had long been social rivals, which did not help towards a peaceful settlement when the brunette collided with the other and grabbed wildly, tearing the left shoulder of a new, latest style dress. Giving an angry squeal, the third girl, a beautiful and shapely red-head, let fly with a slap to the jaw already sore from Jacqueline's kick, setting the brunette back on her heels, and following it up with a grab for the hair which started yet a third battle.

Like the ripples stirred up by a stone thrown into a pond, the fight spread across the room. Excitement had reached the pitch Madam Darcel feared it might as the blonde socialite's fight with the saloongirl started other battles. On the dais one of the brunette's escorts sprang forward meaning to grab hold of the red-head. That brought the second party's male members into the fray and a rousing battle began upon the upper-crust's country.

"Looks like you've got trouble on your hands, Madam," drawled Killem, shoving aside Tophet Tombes as the scout tied into a burly city man who had earlier made some insulting remarks about Calamity's fighting prowess.

"Help me, Dobe!" replied the big woman, swinging a blow which felled a riverboat man before he could tangle with Chan Sing. "Head across that way and make for the door. You'll see a policeman on the street. Yell and tell him there's a riot in here. He'll know what to do. I'll try to make it the other way."

"You're on," grinned the freighter, taking up Calamity's clothing and slouching off on his rescue mission, felling anyone who tried to block his path.

Madam Darcel paused long enough to order her employees, such as were not already involved in the fighting, to protect the merchandise and more expensive fixtures. All around her fights broke out, a wild brawl where one tied into the nearest person and, other than showing a desire to join the fun, meant nothing by doing so. Cursing as tables overturned, chairs shattered and glassware broke, Madam Darcel tried to force her way through to the door. The fighting blonde and saloongirl blocked her way and she threw aside her rules for the correct treatment of the carriage-trade. Shooting out her hands, Madam grabbed each dishevelled girl by the neck, cracked their heads together hard and dropped their limp bodies to the floor. Then she backhanded a man aside and tried to get through the crush so as to be able to summon aid in ending the riot that threatened to wreck her room.

On the dais Calamity and Jacqueline joined battle again after dealing with the socialite interference. Diving forward, Calamity tackled Jacqueline around the waist and rammed the girl backwards. Locked together they crashed into the protective rail, shattered it and fell to the floor. However, Jacqueline was tiring, for she had performed her speciality act twice that evening. On the other hand Calamity's champagne-dousing had partially revived her and her extra weight wore on her opponent. For all that, the fight went on until they reached the wall by the main entrance. Shoving Jacqueline back to the wall, Calamity uncorked a roundhouse swing as the slim girl bounced off. Even as Jacqueline drew back a foot for a kick, she walked full into the punch. Give Calamity her due, she knew how to throw a fist. The blow carried Calamity's weight behind it and Jacqueline helped by walking into it. Back snapped the slim girl's head, her body crashed into the wall, her eyes glazed over and she sank slowly to the floor.

A chair whizzed by Calamity's head and crashed into the wall. Whirling, she stood as well as she could and stared at the brawl taking place before her. More, she saw Madam Darcel emerge from the crowd and formed the wrong idea of the saloonkeeper's motives.

To be fair, Madam Darcel's only intention was to reach the door and summon assistance before the riot went too far. However, she had neither the time nor the inclination to explain such things to Calamity at that moment. Instead she clenched her right hand, throwing it at Calamity's head. Happen Calamity had been her usual self instead of all tuckered out from as rough a brawl as she could remember, she could have easily avoided the blow. In her present exhausted state, Calamity moved too slowly and the fist crashed into the side of the girl's jaw, depositing her in a heap on top of Jacqueline. As blackness came down on her, Calamity wondered if the roof *had* caved in upon her head.

Pain throbbed through Calamity as consciousness returned to her. The roots of her hair felt as if on fire; her left eye throbbed and she reckoned it would have a marvellous mouse under it come morning; while her nose felt twice its usual size, she knew that to be a normal reaction under the circumstances; for the rest, her bruised, grazed body seemed to send stabs of agony from different points in rotation. Slowly she raised a hand to her jaw and groaned. Then she realised that her clothing appeared to be soaking wet.

Making an effort, Calamity opened her eyes. The first thing to meet her gaze was the sight of Killem and that fancy city lawman, St. Andre looking down in some concern at her.

"Are you all right, *cherie?*" asked St. Andre worriedly.

"Only time I felt better was when a hoss throwed me, walked over me, then tossed me into a bobcat's nest with its hooves," Calamity answered, after manipulating her jaw gently to make sure it still worked. "Where was you when I needed you, Sherry?"

"I came as soon as I heard, my pet. But I found you sleeping like a babe."

Before Calamity could think up a suitable reply, she glanced at the room and what she saw drove the thought from her mind. Everybody and everything appeared to be soaking and no longer showed any inclination to fight. Firemen coiled a couple of hoses nearby and Calamity saw why Latour Street maintained the extra large horse-troughs.

"That's how we end trouble down here, *cherie,*" St. Andre went on, following her line of thought. "When this kind of trouble starts, the police bring a fire engine along to damp the fighters' ardour."

"Then why in hell didn't they come in sooner and damp that skinny gal's ardour, whatever it might be. That gal'd got ardour to spare and sure needed it damping down a mite—Hey, where is she?"

Trying to rise, Calamity looked around her. She found Jacqueline to be still out cold, but a couple of saloongirls tended to the slim dancer. Across the room Madam Darcel went among the crowd, holding out a derby hat into which men dropped cash donations to help pay for the damage caused by their fighting. Forcing herself to her feet, Calamity shook off Killem and St. Andre's restraining hands, then walked slowly across the room towards the saloonkeeper.

"Come on boys!" Madam called, offering the hat to the red-headed socialite's friends as they escorted the girl towards the door. "You've had your fun and I've got damage to pay for."

"Talking about money, Madam," Calamity put in.

Slowly Madam Darcel turned and looked Calamity over. "Were we talking about money?"

"If we weren't, we sure as hell soon will be. I figure me 'n' and the gal went at it for ten minutes. At five dollars a minute, according to a half-smart lil Western gal like me, that's fifty dollars you owe me."

Before any more could be said, the red-haired socialite whispered to her escort and took some money which he removed from his billfold. All the trio bore marks of the battle, the men in soaking, rumpled suits, minus neck-ties and with shirts torn; the girl sporting a black eye, swollen lip and a couple of scratches, while her cloak did not entirely cover the fact that her dress had taken some hard pulling and needed holding up with one hand. However, despite all that the girl gave a friendly smile as she came towards Calamity and held out the money.

"I hope you won't be offended at this gift," she told Calamity. "For years I wished to get my fingers into that cat Celestine's hair, and you did what I have long wished to do to Paulette."

"Thanks," answered Calamity, accepting the five ten dollar bills. "You did all right yourself once you got started."

"I must admit it was fun while it lasted, though I don't know what Papa will say when he hears."

With that the red-head joined her two male friends and after each man slipped a donation into Madam's hat, they left the room. Calamity watched them go, a grin on her face. It looked like those fancy-dress dude Frenchmen were some hecats when a fuss started; but she already knew that from her earlier meeting with St. Andre. Anyways, business came first and Madame Darcel still had not made good her promise of remuneration.

"Hey, Madam," Calamity said, turning her attention to the saloonkeeper once more. "How's about the money? I'd hate like hell to have to come in tomorrow night and ask for it again."

"I believe you would come again tomorrow," said Madam Darcel. "Just as I now believe you *are* Calamity Jane."

"I never doubted *that* for a teensey minute," grinned Calamity and held out her right hand. "Fifty dollars, I'll take it in tens."

With a broad smile, Madam Darcel counted off fifty dollars and handed it to Calamity. "I'm almost tempted not to pay. Your fight was a good attraction. But I don't believe the police would go for two riots in a week at my place."

"I'll mind that, if I come tonight. Anyways, you couldn't get another gal as tough as that skinny kid. See you up the trail, Madam."

Crossing the floor. Calamity made straight for where Jacqueline had been helped to her feet by the other girls. Seeing her opponent approaching, Jacqueline shook the other girls' hands from her and prepared to defend herself. St. Andre also expected trouble and started to move forward. A huge hand closed on his arm and held him back despite the fact that the detective was no weakling himself.

"Don't bother, friend," said Killem's gentle voice. "Calam's not fixing to cause fuss."

"Hey there, easy," Calamity stated, holding her hands hip high and spread with open palms towards Jacqueline in the Indian peace sign. "We raised enough lumps on each other for one night. How'd you feel, sk—gal. Which same, I reckon you feel just about as sick and sore as I do."

"I'm all right."

"Yeah, I tell lies too," grinned Calamity and counted out fifty dollars.

"What's that for?" Jacqueline asked, staring at the money.

"Your cut. I sure as hell couldn't have won it without you."

"But—but—."

Letting out a mock serious sigh, Calamity said, "Don't tell me I've got to lick you again afore you'll take it."

"Are you serious?" gasped Jacqueline.

"I'm allus serious where money's concerned, sk—gal."

Wondering what kind of girl she had met, Jacqueline accepted the money. She tried to express her thanks, but Calamity laughed them off. At that moment Madam Darcel arrived and gave her girls orders to take Jacqueline to their quarters so a doctor could examine her injuries.

"And you, Calamity, he'll examine you also," the saloon-keeper went on.

"Shucks no. I've broken nothing," Calamity scoffed. "I'll just rub on some of my soothing syrup and I'll be fit as frog's hair comes morning." Then, knowing something of saloonkeepers' ways when dealing with their employees, she decided to hand out a warning. "I shared the money with sk—Jacqueline here. It's for *her*, Madam, understand?"

Madam Darcel understood all too well. Strangely she felt no resentment at Calamity's words or what they implied, but took them as the girl meant, as an interest in seeing Jacqueline received fair dealing.

"You'd best be getting home, Calam," Killem remarked. "Don't want you all stove up with a chill comes morning."

"Or me," agreed Calamity, then studied her employer closely. "Hey, how come you aren't wet?"

"When the fuss started, I got out and yelled for help."

"Spoilsport!" sniffed Calamity.

"Anyways, I saved your coat, hat and bandana from a wetting."

"Thanks too much! Why didn't you leave them and save me?"

"Shucks, gal, I saw you enjoying yourself with that Jacqueline gal and didn't want to bill in."

"One of these days, Dobe Killem," Calamity began, "I'm going to tell everybody your name's—well what we both know it is."

Killem suffered under the given name of Cecil, a fact Calamity alone of his outfit knew. When her boss grew obstreperous, she used the knowledge to bring him back into line.

"And what is Dobe's name?" asked an interested Madam Darcel.

Thrusting the coat, hat and bandana into Calamity's hands, Killem gave a warning growl. "You tell her and I'll peel your hide. Get off home and leave me to round up the rest of the boys."

"May I escort Calamity home, sir?" asked St. Andre stepping forward and remembering the girl's statement that her boss and fellow workers treated her like their sister.

However, he need not have taken the trouble. With a grin, Killem nodded to the girl. "Try asking her, friend. She'll damned soon say 'yes' or 'no'."

"Let's go, Sherry," Calamity said.

"Tuck your shirt in first and put on your coat, preferably with the buttons fastened," replied St. Andre.

For the first time Calamity realised that at some point in the fight every button had been torn from the front of her shirt and its flap hung outside her pants. Showing no embarrassment, she made the necessary adjustments to her dress and finally pulled on her coat. Having worn a man's vest under the shirt, Calamity knew she showed little that might raise eyebrows in polite society. Winking at Killem, she accepted St. Andre's arm and walked from the *Cheval D'Or*.

At the end of Latour Street, St. Andre hailed a passing cab. He helped Calamity inside, then gave the driver instructions and swung up to sit by the girl. On the ride to the local station house, where they collected Calamity's gunbelt and Navy Colt, St. Andre learned the cause of the fight.

"Madam Darcel's honest, Calamity," he told the girl. "She wouldn't allow a pickpocket in her place—not for long anyway."

"That one sure didn't stop," agreed Calamity. "Say, that Jacqueline was one tough kid. Was them kicks she gave me that *sa—savate*, or whatever you call it?"

"It was. I've seen Jacqueline at Duval's and at the *Cheval D'Or*, she's good, very good."

Putting a hand to her nose, Calamity winced slightly. "I'll take your word for it."

Not until the cab circled the edge of City Park did either Calamity or St. Andre mention the murder. However, while listening to Calamity's discourse on the subject of Jacqueline's fighting prowess, an idea began to form in St. Andre's head. No matter how hard he tried to force the thoughts down, they kept recurring, nagging at him, yet he did not put them into words.

"What happened about the gal who got killed?" Calamity asked, glancing out of the cab's window.

"I'm on the case now. Caiman has gone down with a convenient bout of fever and the Chief of Police put me in charge."

"You're a real lucky feller."

"I wouldn't say so. Both the *Picayune* and the *Intelligencer* are after somebody's blood over the failure to trap the Strangler. Unless he is caught soon, I fear my head will roll."

"Which same'd be a right shame," remarked Calamity. "We'd best start to think how we'll lay hands on him."

Although he relapsed into silence, St. Andre thought only indirectly about trapping the Strangler. On a visit to the *Cheval D'Or*, he had seen Jacqueline meet and defeat another skilled *savate* fighter. Knowing more than a little about foot-boxing himself, St. Andre could figure how rough tangling with Jacqueline was likely to be. Yet Calamity did tangle and defeated the slim girl. St. Andre already knew how tough and capable Calamity could act. Such a girl might—he let the rest of the thought trail off unused. Such a thing had never been done before, the risks were too great for him even to suggest his idea.

St. Andre moved restlessly and gave a low grunt of pain as his sore body protested.

"Aching a mite?" asked Calamity turning to look at him.

"I'll be as stiff as a plank in the morning."

"Got me a real good cure for that, happened you'd like to try it."

"*Cherie*, I would try anything. It is not good for a lawman to be stiff."

"You can say that again," grinned Calamity.

So St. Andre found himself once more in Calamity's room, seated on her bed and watching her bring a small bottle full of an oily-looking liquid from her medicine bag. Drawing the cork with her teeth and spitting it aside, she walked towards the detective.

"This's something an old Pawnee witch-woman whomped up for me," she said. "Take off your jacket, vest, shirt and that fancy undershirt I bet you wear."

68

While St. Andre did not lead the life of a Trappist monk, he felt slightly embarrassed by the girl's calm request that he stripped to the waist.

"You mean now?" he gasped.

"Naw, in a week, after I've gone back up-river. You don't drink this stuff. It gets rubbed on the hurt part and I can't do that with your clothes on. And don't get all modest, I've seen a feller's hairy chest afore today."

Deciding he may as well give in, St. Andre stripped to the waist. Without any blushing, simpering, or showing any more than casual interest in the muscular exposed torso, Calamity sat him on the bed. Pouring some of the liquid into the palm of her hand, she carefully applied it to the bruised skin. Whatever the liquid might be—and St. Andre feared to ask—it worked fast, soothing and cooling the ache from his bones and flesh.

"You're a wonder, Calam," he said when she finished.

"Why sure," she agreed, then flexing her arms. "Whooee, I'm sore."

Was there a hint of challenge in her voice, St. Andre wondered.

"Miss Canary's soothing syrup did me good," he remarked.

"It's sure hell to put on yourself," she answered. "Hell, my clothes are wet. I've got to get out of them."

Rising, she peeled off the shirt and vest, standing with her back to him. Even so, a mottling of bruises showed on her ribs as she dropped the clothes on to a chair.

"Calam—," St. Andre began. "Can we talk?"

"Know for sure I can, and I've heard you doing it all fancy and nice."

"Then sit by me, I'll put some of that stuff on for you and we'll talk."

# CHAPTER EIGHT

### Miss Canary's Suggestion

DAYLIGHT streamed through the window as St. Andre drew the curtains. Stepping to one side, he flexed his arms and marvelled at the ease with which he could move. By all fair means he ought to be so stiff and sore that even the smallest movement caused agony, yet he felt relaxed and almost his normal self. Behind him the bed creaked and he turned to study Calamity's sleep twisted face showing over the blankets.

"How are your injuries, *cherie?*" he asked, crossing to sit by her.

Hooking a hand behind his neck, Calamity drew his face down and kissed him. "Shucks, don't feel a thing," she answered when they parted. "What'd you want to talk about last night?"

Looking down at the girl as she lay so innocently on the bed, St. Andre did not answer for several seconds. Last night while applying Miss Canary's soothing syrup to Calamity's injuries he had thought of making use of the girl's undoubted courage and unusual talents to trap the Strangler. Now in the cold light of dawn, and after a night which proved beyond any doubt that Calamity *was* all woman, the idea no longer seemed possible. His plan would be too dangerous for any woman to risk her life trying it out.

Seeing the girl's lips tighten in a way he guessed meant she aimed to have the question answered, St. Andre forced himself to think fast.

"I was thinking about your suggestion that your friend tries to track the Strangler," he answered, using the first lie to come into his head.

His attempt at a bluff missed by a good country mile. Looking the detective over with calculating eyes, Calamity grinned and said, "What'd you do if I called you a liar?"

"Why not try it and see?" he challenged.

Calamity tried it; and saw.

Half an hour later, as he finished dressing, St. Andre felt even more certain that he could never put his plan into operation and risk Calamity's life. Hoping to evade the issue, he felt at the stubble on his cheeks and remarked that he needed a shave.

"Go down and get some breakfast," Calamity told him. "The boys'll be in the dining-room by now and one of 'em'll loan you his razor."

Although he did not feel sure of what kind of reception he would receive from the members of Killem's freight outfit, St. Andre followed the girl's advice and headed for the dining-room. Inside he found the members of the outfit sat around the clean, well-stocked table. All eyes turned towards him as he entered the room; but, much to his surprise, he found grins, not indignation or fury on the freighters' faces.

The way Killem and his men looked at the present situation was that none of them had the right to censure Calamity's morals. Even the married members of the outfit took female company when away from home on a trip, so none of them expected Calamity to sit alone and nun-like while they whooped things up. She did not throw herself at every man who came along, and the old Pawnee medicine woman had fixed up something which enabled Calamity to make sure that nothing permanent happened as a result of her friendship. In the final reckoning, the freighters allowed any man who became *that* friendly with their Calamity-gal must be all he-cat and well worth knowing—even if he be a town-dwelling, fancy-dressing and talking French-Creole aristocrat and a lawman to boot.

"Bring on another breakfast, maw!" called Dobe Killem as the owner of the apartment house looked in. "This young feller done stayed the night with us and he looks a mite hungry."

While St. Andre was not used to having four eggs and a pile of ham placed before him at breakfast, he tucked in and demolished the lot; which brought broad grins and friendly chaff from the freighters.

"Never did see a feller as could eat so much," remarked Killem.

"They do say *it* makes a man real hungry," Tombes went on.

"I missed dinner last night," St. Andre explained.

At that moment Calamity entered and St. Andre thrust back his chair to come to his feet. Much to his surprise none of the other men broke into ill-mannered comment on his show of etiquette. While they might be a mite long on the social graces themselves, Killem's outfit never mocked anybody whose early training gave him polite manners and habits.

"Morning, boys, hi Sherry," greeted Calamity innocently. "Say, did you come back here last night?"

"Reckon he must have," grinned the owner of the house,

guessing the girl's words had been aimed in her direction. "You ready for breakfast?"

"Ready, willing and all set to eat it, maw," agreed Calamity, then turned to Tombes. "Hey, Tophet, happen you can see two inch afore your nose, Sherry here wants you to help trail that Strangler cuss."

"And we got them hosses to tend to," Killem went on. "I'll loan you my razor when you're through, Sherry."

By the time he had washed, shaved and tidied up his appearance as well as possible, St. Andre found he possessed a new name. It stuck and for the rest of his life St. Andre's friends called him 'Sherry'.

Calamity made no reference to the question she knew hovered around in St. Andre's head and which he fought down each time before speaking. Figuring the detective would get around to asking in his own good time, Calamity shared a cab with St. Andre and a silent, morose-looking Tombes, and rode to City Park. After St. Andre paid off the cab, the trio strolled through the Park. In daylight it looked different; innocent, friendly, not the kind of area one would associate with a brutal murder.

A couple of policemen stood guard on the place where the body had lain. Both of them exchanged glances as they watched St. Andre's party approaching.

"There's a feller whose job I'd hate to have," remarked one of the officers.

"And me," replied the other. "Anyway, he's got plenty of money and don't need this lot to live on."

Saluting St. Andre, the two policemen fell back, wondering why he had brought that mean-looking cuss and a gal wearing men's clothing along to the scene of the crime. Not that they objected in Calamity's case, she sure filled out that pair of blue jeans a treat. Neither officer wasted any time in asking questions, but stood back and awaited orders.

"What do we do now?" the detective asked.

"Just stand right back and don't get under-foot," grunted Tombes, never too amiable first thing in a morning, and less so when recovering from the previous night's celebration. "I sure hope your fellers haven't been tromping every damned which ways down here."

"I left orders for them to stay on the path."

After making a check on the ground at the left of the track, Tombes returned to the detective and nodded. "They done what you telled 'em. Ain't nothing aged right on that side. I'll look on the other."

St. Andre had never seen a human tracker in action and looked on with mingled interest and disbelief as the lean Westerner advanced towards the right side of the track and bent forward so as to study the grass. Possibly they would learn nothing through the scout's efforts, but St. Andre knew Calamity had not been joking when she made the suggestion.

A low grunt left Tombes' lips as he came to a halt, bent closer to the ground and examined something which caught his eye. Then he stood erect and turned to face Calamity and St. Andre.

"Feller come along the path with the gal."

"Could you tell me how you know, so I can write it in my report," St. Andre answered.

"Easy enough," grunted the scout. "There's a set of tracks that's the right age comes off the path here. Just the one set. Happen she'd come along the path alone, he'd've left sign in the bushes where he waited for her and walked out to stop her. After he'd killed her, he walked off into the bushes over there."

"Couldn't both the Strangler and the girl have come from the bushes?" St. Andre inquired.

"Nope. There's only the one set of tracks, going on to the grass and through the bushes."

"And you say he walked away?"

"Sure, Sherry. It's easy enough to tell the difference. Come here and take a look at his sign."

Bending forward, the scout pointed to the grass. Only by careful study could St. Andre see anything different from the spot at which Tombes pointed and the surrounding area. Even when seeing that a small oval-shaped patch of grass had been crushed down, he could not decide how Tombes knew the Strangler made the indentation when walking away from his victim. Seeing the detective's puzzled expression, and knowing how little chance the average city-dweller had of watching a visual tracker at work, Tombes explained his findings.

"Look at the shape of the mark," he said. "When a man walks, he puts his heel down first, brings the rest of his foot down. But when he runs, he lands on the toe. With walking you get a bigger mark than when he's running. The amount the crushed grass's come up tells me how long ago the sign was made."

"I'll take your word for that," St. Andre answered admiringly.

"You can sure do that," Calamity put in, conscious of the two patrolmen studying her shape with anything but official interest.

"Ole Tophet can track a man across rock by the marks his shadow left on it. Mind though, it has to be fairly soft rock—and a *real* sunny day"

"What would you do if I called you a liar, *cherie?*" smiled St. Andre.

"Nothing right now. I reckon you've got all kinds of laws against doing *that* in the open. Let's leave it until later and get after ole Tophet."

"What the hell's all this about, Mike?" one of the patrolmen asked in a low voice as they watched Tombes, then Calamity and St. Andre move away.

"Don't ask me," grunted the other. "Say, I wonder who worked St. Andre over?"

"That girl's got a mouse under her eye. Maybe it was her."

"Naw. St. Andre charms 'em, he don't beat 'em until they're ready for it. I reckon we'd best tag along and see what happens."

"Be as well. If we stay here we'll be in the wrong, and if we follow it'll be the same, but at least we might learn something."

Moving slowly, his eyes scanning the ground ahead of him, Tombes led the others through the bushes. Calamity kept her attention on the route they took, noticing that the Strangler's direction was such that it never came into plain view of a path but made a looping half-circle in cover. Just as she was about to remark on the matter, Tombes halted and looked back at St. Andre.

"Feller's around five foot ten tall, slim build, wears city shoes," the scout stated.

"How do you know?" asked the detective.

"Easy enough. Length of his stride, amount he crushed down the grass, shape of a couple of real clear tracks he left. Which same don't help you much, I reckon."

"At least it eliminates a lot of people. Where did he go from here?"

All the time they walked St. Andre had been studying the direction they took and noting it in his memory. If they ever caught the Strangler after a killing, it might be possible to shock a confession from him by describing the route he took from one of his victims.

After following the tracks for another fifty yards, Tombes came to a halt. He stood at the edge of a clump of bushes, looking around him. On joining the scout, Calamity and St. Andre found themselves overlooking a piece of track and the girl particularly developed an uneasy feeling she knew the place which lay before them.

"What is it?" asked St. Andre, now convinced that Tombes had done all Calamity promised.

"Feller stood here for a fair spell, looking towards the path," Tombes answered. "I'll cross over and see what's on the other side. He went this ways, come on to the path here." However, after crossing the path and searching around, the scout returned to the others. "That's as far as we go. Feller didn't cross the track on to the other side and I can't trail him on this hard ground."

Interested though they had been up to that point, Calamity and St. Andre hardly heard a word Tombes said. Both stood staring at the bullet-holed top hat which lay on the ground ahead of them. Then they turned and their eyes met.

"He must've been stood here last night, watching us," Calamity breathed.

"If the newspapers hear of this," replied St. Andre. "I'm finished as a policeman."

"Can't see why," the girl answered. "Hell, who'd've expected the Strangler to come here and stand watching us? You couldn't have known about him."

"My dear child," said St. Andre gently. "The *Intelligencer* has never approved of the police, or my rise through its ranks. They will be only too pleased to make capital of this incident."

"Why don't you go along to their office, ask the boss to walk out into the alley and talk some sense to him with that there *savate*?" asked the practical Miss Canary.

"It is not as easy as that, *cherie*," the detective answered a touch regretfully. "You see the *Intelligencer* is a protector of the rights of the down-trodden, under-privileged mankind, and its owners have a very stout idea of how to gain full protection from the law for their actions."

Before St. Andre could enlarge on the working of a newspaper like the *Intelligencer*, Tombes returned to them and jerked his thumb towards the track.

"I've been down both sides and he didn't go off again near at hand. Reckon from the way he come off the grass, he was headed down that ways."

"Towards the better part of town," answered St. Andre. "Of course he would hardly, come the other way. We'd just gone along there. Well, that's all we can do for now."

"Hope I helped some," Tombes replied.

"You've given us a little more than we already knew," St.

Andre said. "I'm grateful for your help. Let's go back to town."

"What's your next move?" Calamity inquired, after collecting the discarded top hat.

"We wait," St. Andre told her.

"Just wait?"

"That's all we can do."

"Hell!" spat the girl. "He might kill again."

"He might," admitted St. Andre, "but until we have something to go on, we can't think of catching him."

"Do you know who the girl was?" asked Calamity.

"Not even that. People in her way of business avoid the law as I told you last night—."

"That feller acts like a stock-killing cougar," Tombes interrupted. "Ain't but two ways of hunting down one of them. Run him down with a pack of hounds, or stake out a bait and lure him to your gun."

"Now there's a right smart idea, Sherry." Calamity put in. "Get a gal to act as bait for you."

For a few seconds St. Andre did not reply. He walked along between Tombes and Calamity, the patrolmen following on his heels, his head sunk forward and thoughts racing through his mind. At last he shrugged and looked at the girl.

"We have three police matrons at Headquarters, but I doubt if they would be of any use as bait. All the Strangler's victims were shapely and good-looking girls, at least we assume they were good looking, their distorted faces give little clue of that. Our matrons are all bigger, and not so handsome as Dobe Killem."

"Shucks," answered Calamity, not looking at the detective. "I'm a mite smaller and a whole heap prettier than ole Dobe. Why not let me be your bait?"

"You?" asked St. Andre, trying to sound as if the idea had not been beating around in his head for the past few hours.

"G'wan!" grinned Calamity. "You've been fixing to ask me to do it ever since last night."

St. Andre slammed to a halt, turning and staring at the girl with dismay on his face. Seeing the grin on her face, a smile fought its way to his features, then died off once more.

"It could be very dangerous, *cherie*," he warned.

"Did you ever drive a six-hoss Conestoga wagon through hostile Injun country, Sherry?" she countered. "You might say that's dangerous too—I've done it."

Resuming walking again, St. Andre watched the girl's face. His thoughts turned over the idea which had played back and forth since the previous night, trying to decide how justified he was in endangering Calamity's life.

"We could have men following you," he finally said, then shook his head. "No! It's too much of a chance!"

"Reckon I'm the best judge of that," she answered.

"Reckon you just might as well give up and let her do it, Sherry," warned Tombes. "Ole Calam's done made her mind to be the bait, so she'll do with or without your help."

"Which same it'll be safer with your help," the girl pointed out. "Look, Sherry, I know how dangerous it'll be and I'm still game to give it a whirl if you are."

"It might work," admitted St. Andre. "But you would have to dress for the part. One sees few street-walkers dressed in men's clothing."

"You mean I'd have to put on a dress and all?" gasped Calamity.

"And all," agreed the detective.

Calamity let out a long, suffering sigh. Here was an aspect of the affair her impetuous nature failed to notice when forming the plan. Such an important decision might have taken some girls a long time to settle, but not Calamity. She stiffened her shoulders and looked at St. Andre.

"All right," she said in the tone of a martyr agreeing to be tossed to the lions. "I'll even wear a dress, happen it'll nail the Strangler."

"Let's go somewhere and make our arrangements," St. Andre suggested.

"How about those four jaspers who worked you over?" Calamity inquired.

"I have feelers out for them, but the Strangler case is of more importance right now."

Finding a cab, St. Andre took his party across town to Police Headquarters, a large old stone building which did not resemble any lawman's office Calamity or Tombes had ever seen. The Detective Bureau occupied the second floor and St. Andre's small room faced the Captain of Detectives' quarters. After seeing his superior and explaining his idea, then being granted permission to try it out, St. Andre took Calamity and Tombes into his office where they started to plan their campaign.

First St. Andre called in four men to act as escort when Calamity went out as bait. They would work in plain clothes instead of uniform and were not known in the Latour Street area. Supplying Calamity with the correct clothing for the part offered no difficulties. However, there were snags.

"How well does Calamity know the area?" asked Redon, the shortest of the escort and its senior member.

"I don't," Calamity admitted.

"That may be difficult." Redon stated. "We can't be too close to her—."

"Hey!" interrupted Calamity. "I know somebody who might be able to help."

"Who?" asked St. Andre.

"That skinny gal I fought last night, Jacqueline. I bet she'd jump at the chance of helping."

St. Andre shook his head. "I don't know about that."

"Then let's go ask her," Calamity suggested. "She can only say 'no'."

Rising, St. Andre prepared to leave the room. He told his men to collect their clothing and meet him at his office after lunch. Then he started for the door with Calamity and Tombes at his side. Suddenly the detective came to a halt.

"I've just thought of something, Calam!"

"Such as?"

"The Strangler saw you last night, and with me. He might recognise you."

"He might at that," agreed the girl. "It's something else we'll have to think about."

# CHAPTER NINE

## Miss Canary Acts As Bait

DOBE Killem saw the flashily-dressed blonde girl standing before the open door of Maw Packer's apartment house and felt surprised. While the *Rue de la Paix* could not be classed on the same social level as Bourbon or Toulouse Streets, it was not an area frequented by young ladies of that type.

While walking towards the blonde, Killem studied her, deciding she looked vaguely familiar. She had a nice figure that a cheap, gaudy blue dress revealed rather than concealed, sported the usual parasol and reticule of her kind and wore a large-brimmed hat on her blonde hair. Figuring she might be one of the girls his party entertained at the *Cheval D'Or* the previous evening, Killem nodded as he went by her. Killem decided he would find out which of the outfit invited her over and request that the one involved refrained from bringing calico cats to the house.

"You getting too rich and high-toned to talk with the hired help, Cecil?" asked Calamity's voice.

Although Killem had a well-deserved reputation for being a real good poker player who rarely showed his emotions, he came to a halt as if running into an invisible wall. His mouth dropped open as he turned to stare at the flashily-dressed blonde. For a moment he thought his ears had played a trick on him, then slowly Calamity's face formed out of the blonde curls and make-up.

"What—!" he croaked. "How—."

"Shut your mouth afore you get flies in it," grinned the delighted Calamity and looked towards the door of the building. "I'd say it works, Sherry."

Seeing a couple of thin, pinched, sanctimonious faces peeking from behind the curtains of a house across the street, Killem gave a low angry grunt. His eyes took in the girl's appearance again, noting that the heavy make-up she wore all but hid the mouse she carried under her left eye. However, standing in front of a house on the respectable *Rue de la Paix* was hardly the place to start asking questions about his employee's appearance.

"Let's get off the street!" he growled.

"Scared I'll ruin you socially, Cecil?" inquired Calamity with a mischievous and merry grin.

"I'll ruin you!" the freighter spat out.

Bobbing a curtsy to the watching women, and causing a hurried disappearance behind the curtains, Calamity grabbed hold of Killem's arm. Giving an annoyed grunt, Killem tried to pull himself free of the girl's grip, but she hung on all the more as they headed towards the door of the Packer house.

"What's wrong, Cecil?" she grinned. "Ashamed of being seen with me?"

"Damn your ornery, fool hide, Calam!" Killem snarled back. "I'll take a switch to your butt!"

"Which same I wouldn't feel it through this bustle," answered the girl, hauling him into the hall of the house. "I bet old Nosey and her pard over yonder are getting some right smart ideas of what's going to happen now."

"And me!" snapped Killem.

While Killem enjoyed a piece of rough-and-tumble good fun as much as the next man, he felt that Calamity had gone a whole heap too far this time. To his way of thinking, a practical joke should only cause discomfort to the participants and not bring embarrassment on innocent heads. New Orleans, even this poorer section of the old city, had advanced beyond the rough-and-ready Western town Calamity knew. Calamity's joke might bring down repercussions on Maw Packer's head when the two watchers across the street spread word that she allowed street-walkers to make use of her premises.

On entering the hall, Killem found not only St. Andre but Maw Packer standing facing the door. Instead of being furious at Calamity's behaviour, the woman grinned broadly.

"How'd it go?" Maw asked.

"He walked right by me," answered Calamity proudly. "Acted all honourable and up-right like a deacon going down a cat-house street. Never gave me more than a look-but-don't-touch look."

"Just what the hell's all this about?" demanded Killem in a hoarse bellow. "Damned if I don't—."

Then he stopped, staring at Calamity, and began to roar with laughter. On entering the house Calamity had stepped clear of her boss and removed the hat and blonde wig which so altered her appearance. For a moment Calamity stared at her employer, then swung towards Maw and St. Andre who both joined in the merriment.

"What's so funny? she yelled.

"L—Look in the mirror, *cherie!*" St. Andre managed to get out through his laughter.

Calamity followed his advice and looked into the hat-stand mirror. A reflected vision greeted her and she saw the cause of her friend's laughter. While the heavy make-up and long, glistening pendant earrings had been in keeping with the picture-hat and blonde curls, they looked incongruous framed by her mop of short natural red hair.

"Land-sakes!" she gasped, after joining in the laughter. "I'll sure have to keep my shop-bought white scalp on all the time. Say, Maw. those two old pills across the way were like to swallow their teeth when they saw me haul Dobe in here."

"It'll give 'em something to talk about," Maw answered calmly. "I can allus quieten them down by threatening to give the Reverend Postle all their sassafrass tea."

"Now me," Calamity remarked. "I'd be more likely to keep quiet happen you told me you'd make me *drink* sassafrass tea."

"So would they, only they flavour their tea with maybe seven-eighths gin."

"How's about somebody telling me what this's all about," suggested Killem.

"Let's go into the dining-room and I'll explain," St. Andre replied.

In the dining-room, seated at the table with cups of coffee before them, St. Andre started to explain the reason for Calamity's disguise.

On their arrival at the *Cheval D'Or*, Calamity and St. Andre interviewed Jacqueline and the *savate*-fighting ballet dancer agreed to help all she could on hearing they planned to try to trap the Strangler. However, she stated that she felt Calamity would not be able to pass herself off as a street-girl with the little aid possible between then and night-fall, there was too much Calamity needed to know for that. Quite calmly Jacqueline offered to go along with Calamity and act as a second piece of bait. In vain St. Andre tried to point out the dangers involved. Jacqueline claimed she could chance anything Calamity risked and the Western girl added her weight to the argument.

The question of clothing came up next, but found an easy solution. Having to obtain permission from Madam Darcel for Jacqueline's absence, St. Andre took the saloonkeeper into his confidence. Immediately Madam Darcel offered every assistance and, without telling the real reason for the request, obtained the loan of clothing which fitted Calamity for her part as a street-walker. Madam also came up with the idea of a blonde wig, without knowing that the Strangler had seen Calamity and St. Andre together, saying the girl would look more in character without that mop of short hair.

Calamity, dressed in her new outfit, returned to Maw Packer's place and had been explaining her actions to a sceptical and suspicious owner when they saw Killem returning from the river-front where he spent the day. Deciding to try out her disguise, Calamity slipped out of the house and awaited her employer's arrival. If Killem's reaction be anything to go on, Calamity doubted whether the Strangler, who only saw her by moonlight and from a distance, would recognise her.

"So you're aiming to use Calam and that Jacqueline gal for bait," said Killem when St. Andre finished his explanation.

"I am," agreed the detective. "But I'll give them every protection."

"You see you do!" warned Killem. "Happen anything goes wrong and that gal is hurt—."

"Dobe honey!" whooped Calamity, throwing her arms around her boss and gave him a kiss. "I didn't think you cared."

"Who says I care?" grunted the freighter, gently standing the girl at arms' length and ruffling her hair. "Only the Army done give me an advance on your pay; and anyways you're such an ornery cuss that happen you got killed you'd come back and haunt me. Danged if you aren't trouble enough alive, without having you around as a haunt."

"Who're you trying to convince?" asked Calamity. "Us—or you?"

Ignoring the question, and not wanting his concern for Calamity's welfare to be too obvious, Killem released the girl and turned to St. Andre. "You want a few of my boys around?"

"I'd rather use my own men," the detective replied. "They know what to do. After all, you wouldn't expect policemen to be able to handle your big wagons."

"Reckon you're right," admitted the freighter. "Say, Calam gal, do you have a gun?"

"I thought of it," replied the girl. "But I don't want to spook the Strangler happen I meet him."

"I doubt if he would chance his games with an armed girl," St. Andre pointed out. "Some of the girls do carry a Derringer in their reticule, but none of the Strangler's victims have had one with her."

Killem frowned. While he knew Calamity to be a girl who knew how to take care of herself, mostly she had either her Navy Colt or bull-whip handy. Dressed in such a manner, she could hardly carry either. The big freighter did not care for the idea of his Calamity tangling with the Strangler unless adequately protected. However, he knew that St. Andre would not endanger Calamity's life if he could find any other way of catching the Strangler, and in making use of the girl as a decoy meant to take every possible precaution to ensure her safety.

"All right, play it your way," he said. "I know you'll do right by our lil gal, Sherry."

"That I'll promise you, Dobe," answered St. Andre. "But you'll not let any of your men butt in."

"I'll see they don't," Killem promised.

That evening, dressed in the cheap finery sported by the type of girl from which the Strangler selected his victims, Calamity and Jacqueline went out into the city as living decoys. Calamity had hoped to see something of New Orleans during her visit and that evening partially got her wish. Not that she saw the stately buildings, coffee-houses, cafes and theatres of the better part of the old French city. If it comes to a point, such places did not interest Calamity. Such an area was not the Strangler's hunting grounds. He picked his victims from the Latour Street district, selecting girls whose disappearance would arouse little comment. So the two girls went from place to place, visiting the gathering spots of the street-walking sisterhood. While Jacqueline had never worked the streets in such a capacity she had many friends who did and learned enough from them to locate their haunts and carry off the impersonation.

Hovering always in the background came Redon and his three men. They never bunched together and dressed in different fashions, but all in a style which blended into the background. Redon looked like a cheap gambler, the others could pass as riverboat hands, water-front workers, or general town dwellers of the lower-income bracket. Under St. Andre's instructions, the four men were not to interfere should a possible suspect attempt to pick up one of the girls. Instead they must trail the man and girl, stay far enough away so as not to scare him off, but close enough to save her should the man be the Strangler looking for another victim. Only by catching the Strangler in the act could they be sure of a conviction; and the girls willingly accepted the danger to their lives to bring this about.

One useful thing had been learned from Tombes' display of

the art of reading signs that morning. Now the hunters knew they could discard all but men of around the five foot ten mark and with slim builds. With that in mind, Calamity and Jacqueline steered clear of such offers as came from men who did not fit into the general area of Tombes' estimation of the Strangler's size and heft.

At about eleven o'clock, two foot-sore girls found themselves in a small but busy saloon at the lower end of Latour Street. Jacqueline wore her hair down, so nobody recognised her as the graceful star performer of the *Cheval D'Or*. Flopping down at a table, the girls looked around the room. So far nobody of the right height and build had propositioned either girl and they were beginning to realise the enormity of the task ahead of them.

"Whooee!" groaned Calamity, working her toes in the borrowed shoes. "My feet hurts like hell."

"And mine," Jacqueline replied and glanced at a coloured waiter who came up. "Two specials, Sam."

"Yes'm. Does you-all work around here regular?"

"Our men've fixed it for us," Jacqueline answered.

"That's all right then. Only there was a big fight along the street last night and the law has passed the word that they don't want no mo' trouble down here for a spell. I'll git you-all's drinks."

"I wonder who was fighting," grinned Calamity as the waiter departed.

"They do say it was a beautiful, slim girl and a fat red-head," Jacqueline replied.

"Easy there, Skinny," warned a smiling Calamity. "You heard what the man said, the law don't want no trouble down here, so I'd hate to lick you again."

"It's lucky the police passed out that order," Jacqueline remarked. "Some of the real girls might have objected to us coming around otherwise."

"Old Sherry thought of everything," commented Calamity.

Knowing that the street-girls were apt to be jealous of intrusion by new girls into their territory, St. Andre caused the official warning to be passed out that the law would not countenance any more brawls down the Latour Street district after the fight in the *Cheval D'Or*. Such a warning carried weight and the regular girls, while watching the newcomers with suspicious eyes, did not try to assert their prior right to trade when Calamity and Jacqueline entered a place of business.

"Let's hope the plan works," Jacqueline said.

"And quick," augmented Calamity. "I hate that coloured water they serve the gals instead of whisky."

During her tour of the seamier side of the city, Calamity had discovered that the street-girls, while expected to drink something as they sat in a saloon waiting for trade, did not consume real intoxicating liquor. Instead, if they so requested, the girls were served with coloured water masquerading as real drinks, but costing much less than the genuine article. That way a girl could appear to be drinking steadily, had an excuse to be in the place, and still stay sober enough to handle the financial side of the business. In return for the service, they were expected to persuade any customer to buy at least one round of drinks before taking him to their business premises.

The waiter returned, placing the glasses before the girls. Dropping his voice confidentially, he said, "If you ladies wants any introductions—."

"We'll keep it in mind," Calamity answered.

Turning, the waiter walked away and the girls exchanged glances. Then Jacqueline stiffened slightly in her seat, staring at the door.

"Just coming in, Calam!" she whispered, although the new arrival could not possibly have heard her at that distance.

Calamity turned her head in a casual manner to look towards the door and at the man who just entered. For his dress, he appeared to be a seaman of some kind—ocean-going vessels used the New Orleans waterfront to discharge their cargoes—and he stood around five foot ten, a slim, wiry young man with a sallow complexion. For a moment he stood at the door, his eyes roaming around the room and studying the various customers at the tables. Finally his gaze came to rest on Calamity and he started to walk across the room.

Coming to her feet, a buxom brunette caught the man's arm and she made the usual suggestion. With an almost angry gesture, he jerked his arm free and continued his way towards Calamity's table. The brunette scowled, but her companion snapped out a reminder about the police's no-trouble order, so she took her seat again.

On reaching Calamity's table, for a moment he did not speak, his eyes on her face. Not by as much as a glance did he even show he knew of Jacqueline's presence. There was something unnerving about his fixed gaze and blank expression.

"Hi," Calamity greeted, looking up as if suddenly aware of the man's presence. You look lonely."

Calamity reckoned to be a better than fair poker player and capable of reading facial emotions. Never had she seen such a look of hatred as passed briefly over the seaman's face, then was replaced by a smile which stopped long clear of his eyes.

"Reckon I could offer you a drink?" he replied.

"I thought you'd never ask. Pull up a chair and take the weight off your feet."

Even as the slim man sat down, the coloured waiter came gliding over to the table and grinned knowingly at Calamity.

"Is you-all wanting wine for the ladies, sah?"

For a moment the sailor did not reply. Instead he sat staring at Calamity with a fixed, unwinking gaze. Jerking his eyes from the girl, the sailor looked at the waiter and answered, "Bring me a beer."

"And the ladies, sah?"

"Go to hell, coon!" the sailor spat out.

"Take it easy, friend," Calamity put in gently. "He's only doing his job."

"Who asked you—!" the sailor began.

"If that's how you feel!" Calamity interrupted. "I'm going."

Shoving back her chair, she started to rise. The angry, hostile eyes followed her, then various emotions warred on the sailor's face. At last he forced a smile to his lips again.

"I'm sorry, M—. I'm real sorry. Only the mate gave me a bad time afore I left the ship and I've been looking to take it out on somebody. Bring wine for the ladies, feller, and buy yourself something."

Yet after the waiter left, the sailor dropped into a moody silence once more. He answered Calamity's comments on the saloon and its crowd with grunts of silence.

"I reckon we'd best be going, Jackie," Calamity remarked.

Once again the threat of departure brought a change to the man. "I'm sorry, Mavis," he said. "I was thinking."

"I like a thinking man," Calamity replied. "Only the name's not Mavis."

The sailor jerked his eyes to Calamity's face, scowling at her. Then a sly grin twisted his lips. "No, it wouldn't be. Where's that feller with the drinks?"

On his return, the waiter put the drinks on the table and in doing so bent so his mouth was close to Calamity's ear. In a low tone, the waiter issued a warning.

"You-all watch that feller, he's got meanness in him."

"I'll mind it," Calamity replied.

While finishing his drink, the sailor managed to sound more friendly. He laughed at a joke Calamity made and she decided that she might as well get down to business. Finishing her drink, she looked at Jacqueline.

"Reckon we'd better be going," she said, then glanced at the sailor. "Unless you've anything in mind."

"How'd you like to take a walk?"

"I never walk with fellers I don't know," Calamity countered. "'Course, if you told me your name, I'd know you."

"Ben Cope."

From the way the sailor spoke, he thought Calamity should know his name. It meant nothing to her and she smiled.

"Hi, Ben. I'm Jane. Let's take our walk now I know you."

"I've got something to do myself," Jacqueline put in. "See you around, Ben."

Cope did not reply, his cold eyes never left Calamity's face as he rose and took her offered arm. Together they left the saloon and Jacqueline looked around for her escort, wanting to tell them that Calamity had a possible taker.

Outside the saloon, Calamity and Cope turned down Latour Street. Cope said little as they walked, but at last they reached the edge of City Park.

"Let's go in here." he said.

"I'd rather go back for a drink," she answered.

Gripping Calamity's arm tighter, Cope growled, "We're going in there, and if you make a squeak, I'll bust your arm."

From the strength in the slim man's fingers, Calamity decided he could make good his threat. So she allowed herself to be steered into the Park and hoped that St. Andre's men were on hand to come to her rescue.

# CHAPTER TEN

## An Attempt On Miss Canary's Life

COLD fear gripped Jacqueline as she watched Calamity leave the room with Cope. Despite the hectic and violent nature of their first meeting, a strong liking had developed between the girls during the afternoon and evening, and the dancer did not want anything to happen to her new friend. Something about Cope scared Jacqueline. It might have been Cope's moody manner, the way he stared at Calamity, or how his smile never reached his eyes. Jacqueline's every instinct warned her that Cope did not go with Calamity for the usual reasons.

Glancing around the room, Jacqueline suddenly became aware that, due to the coming and going of the customers, none of the escort had seen Calamity and Cope leave and did not know that they should be following the couple.

In later years such decoy work would be organised and mistakes avoided by careful planning. But this was probably the first time any police department employed such tactics to trap a criminal, so, having no precedent to guide them, they made mistakes. If the man with Calamity should be the Strangler, the poor positioning of the escort might cost her dearly.

Rising, Jacqueline started across the room in the direction of Redon who stood at the bar. The stocky detective glanced at Jacqueline, then towards Calamity's empty chair. A look of shocked concern came to his face, and he moved forward meaning to contact Jacqueline in the manner of a customer meeting one of the street-girls. From their places around the room, the other members of the escort read the signs and headed for the door.

A hand caught Jacqueline's arm as she walked towards Redon. Swinging around, and trying to pull herself free, she found herself facing a tall, burly riverboat man.

"Hey there, honey-chile," greeted the man. "How's about you 'n' me having a few lil drinks, then going to your place?"

"I—I've already got a man," she replied.

"Forget him—," the man began.

"She doesn't want to forget him," a voice cut in from the side, "so just take your cotton-picking hands offen her."

Redon did not want trouble, but he could not leave Jacqueline in such a position and the girl might know where Calamity and the sailor were headed. So the detective cut in and one glance told him the riverboat man did not like the interruption one little bit.

A grin creased the burly man's face as he studied Redon's clothes and appearance. All the man saw was a typical tinhorn gambler and not a big one at that. He certainly did not intend to surrender the girl to such a man without the other put up a right convincing argument. Reaching out, the riverboat man laid the palm of his big hand on Redon's fancy vest, meaning to thrust the detective aside.

There was no time to argue with the man. Every second wasted put Calamity's life into greater danger. So Redon knew he must act and act fast. Also that he must finish the burly man first go; and he knew how tough a riverboat worker could be. Such a man needed firm handling and stern measures if he was to be stopped without a hell of a fight.

Fortunately, despite his comparative lack of inches, Redon was a very tough lawman and knew a thing or three about the noble art hand-to-hand combat.

Up came Redon's hands, the left securing the man's wrist from the underside, the right slapping on to the man's fingers and pressing them against the fancy gambler's vest. When Redon bent forward at the hips, pain and the danger of broken bones brought the other man to his knees. Releasing his hold, Redon stepped back fast and lashed up his left foot, the toe catching the man full under his jaw. Back snapped the man's head and he sprawled to the floor, limp and unmoving.

"Some folks just don't know when to get tough!" Redon growled, looking around him and waiting for the unconscious man's friends to make a move.

However, the entire business happened so quickly that few if any of the crowd, appeared to realise what had been done. Redon did not give them a chance to find out, but took Jacqueline's arm and headed across the room.

"Calam's gone out with a man!" Jacqueline gasped as they hurried between the tables. "Raoul, I think he's the Stran—."

"Keep your voice down, Jackie!" the detective interrupted. "We don't want everybody to know."

Normally the owner of the saloon would have objected to a stranger mishandling a good customer, especially when the stranger only bought a couple of beers at the bar. However, the police warning about no trouble caused the man to hold his hand especially as the stranger was leaving, and looked like he might take violent objection to any attempt at showing him the error of his ways.

On the street Jacqueline and Redon came to a halt and looked around them. They could see no sign of Calamity and Cope among the crowd using the sidewalk. The remainder of the escort loomed up around Redon and the girl, all showing concern at their failure to adequately cover Calamity.

"He's killed the others in the Park," one man whispered, trying to avoid attracting attention to them.

"Could get to the Park several ways from here," Redon replied. "Split up, take a different way each. Jackie and I'll go down the street. I hope to God we're in time."

"Hurry, Raoul!" Jacqueline gasped, trying to increase her speed as they left the other members of the party. "We must run—."

"No, Jackie!" Redon answered.

For all the urgency of the situation, Redon knew he dare not run along the street. He had no wish to draw attention to himself and running would cause folks to take notice, might even invite pursuit. If the man with Calamity should be the Strangler, and they captured him, Redon did not want the people of the Latour Street district to know of it. Some of the folk in that area either knew or suspected that a missing friend must be a Strangler victim, even if they would not help the police by identifying the bodies, and would have no mercy on the killer. Should word get out that the Strangler had been captured, Redon doubted if he and his men would take in a living prisoner.

Explaining his reasons for not running, Redon held Jacqueline to a steady walk until they left Latour Street and came towards the entrance to City Park. Sick with worry for her friend's safety, Jacqueline stared ahead along the shadowy paths and wondered if they would be in time to prevent Calamity's death.

Calamity allowed the man to steer her along a path through the Park, trying to catch the sound of her escort's footsteps. Nothing but the normal night noises came to her ears, however, as yet she did not worry for she knew the men would not chance coming too close in case they scared off Cope before he made a move.

"Look, friend," she said, realising she ought to do something. "If you're after a free—."

"I'm only after one thing, Mavis," Cope answered.

"Mavis?" Calamity gasped. "Who is she?"

The grip on her arm tightened and Cope's breath came heavier as he snarled, "Don't try to fool me, Mavis. I recognised you as soon as I came into that place. That big hat, the blonde hair."

Suddenly the man swung Calamity around before him. Hatred and worse glowed on his face, and his hands rose towards her throat. Calamity hesitated a vital instant too long. Nothing had ever frightened her so much as did the sight of the man's face. Before she could take positive action, or even scream, the man's fingers clamped on her throat, the thumbs digging into the sides of her adam's apple and cutting off her breath. Panic hit Calamity for a moment as her hands grabbed instinctively at the man's wrists. Her head seemed to be filled with a roaring and throbbing and all she could see was that hideous, twisted, hate-filled mask of a face before her eyes.

Then Calamity regained control of herself. Something screamed a warning to her senses and she knew she must break the hold on her throat. She wasted no time in wondering where the escort might be. All her life Calamity had been self-reliant and that factor saved her life.

Discarding the futile pulling at the man's wrists, for his arms were too strong for her to drag them off by brute force, Calamity prepared to defend herself with a trick Killem taught her.

"You cheap whore, Mavis!" Cope was yelling and Calamity realised he must have been shouting all the time. "You led my wife astray. Now you're going to—."

At which point Calamity acted in her defence. Simultaneously she launched a kick against his shin and placed the palms of her hands on his elbows. For the first time in her life Calamity blessed wearing women's shoes instead of her comfortable moccasins. All that evening she had cursed the shoes which made her unaccustomed feet ache, but at that moment the shoes saved her. A kick delivered when wearing her moccasins would not have hurt anywhere near as much as did those reviled city shoes.

Pain caused Cope to relax his hold slightly, but it proved to be enough. Desperation added strength to Calamity's naturally strong arms. The sudden, unexpected attack on his shin caused Cope to loosen his grip on Calamity's throat and before he could tighten the fingers again, the girl's hands shoved inwards on his elbows. Cope's hands slipped from Calamity's throat and she thrust him backwards a couple of steps. Sucking in air, Calamity stumbled away from Cope. Before she could start to scream for help, as St. Andre warned her to do, Calamity saw Cope leaping at her, his hands reaching towards her throat, that same mad glare in his eyes.

Footsteps pounded on the path behind Cope. Even in his crazy rage, the sound rang a warning note in the man's head. Glancing over his shoulder, Cope saw a man in gambler's clothes and a slim, flashily-dressed girl running towards him. Gasping for breath, Calamity caught her balance and came forward, whipping around her right fist. Cope turned full into the blow, it caught him on the side of the jaw, coming with Calamity's weight behind it.

Staggering backwards under the impact of the blow, Cope clawed up a hand towards his jacket pocket. Redon sprang forward, the short leather-wrapped, lead-weighted police billie he had drawn on entering the park rose in his right hand and came down. Having seen the man reaching for a pocket and possibly a weapon, Redon took no chances. The billie landed on Cope's head and the sailor's hat gave him no protection. With a low moan, Cope crumpled and went down in a limp pile.

Hurdling the fallen body, Redon caught Calamity by the arms as the girl stood swaying.

"Are you all right, Calam?" he asked.

"Sure," replied Calamity—and fainted for the first time in her life.

Redon lowered the girl to the ground. Jacqueline arrived and shoved by the detective to drop at Calamity's side. Gently the dancer raised Calamity's head and rested it on her knees.

"Is she—!" Jacqueline gasped.

"Just a swoon," Redon replied. "She'll be all right in a couple of minutes."

Leaving Jacqueline to tend to Calamity, Redon drew the Bean Giant handcuffs from the inside pocket of his jacket. Even as he bent down to clip the irons on the unconscious sailor's wrists, he heard feet thudding on a path, coming towards him. Looking up, he saw a burly shape approaching and relief hit him as he recognised the newcomer as another member of the escort.

"Heard him yelling," the newcomer announced. "See you— God! He hasn't—."

"No. She's just fainted."

Voices swirled through the mists which clouded Calamity's head, distant yet clear although she could not make any sense of the words.

"Is she all right?" asked one.

"She'd best be," came another. "If anything happened to her, St. Andre'd have my badge at the least."

Shaking her head to clear it, Calamity tried to force herself into a sitting position. Hands gripped her shoulders and held her down. For a moment panic hit her as memory flooded back. Grabbing up, she gripped the wrists of the hands which held her. Then she saw a face above her. A pale, scared face, but not the hate-crazed features of the sailor.

"You—You're hurting, Calam!" Jacqueline gasped.

Only with an effort could Calamity open her fingers. She realised that she lay on her back, her head resting on Jacqueline's knees. Beyond Jacqueline stood Redon and another of the policemen—and to one side, stretched out upon the ground with his wrists secured by handcuffs, even though he would not be going anywhere for a spell, lay Cope.

Calamity stiffened, then fought down a momentary panic and hint of hysteria as she looked at the man and remembered his hate-filled face with the mad eyes glaring at her. Determined not to go 'woman', have hysterics in front of her friends, Calamity fought for and gained control of herself.

"I'm sorry, Jackie," she said and raised a hand to touch her throat.

Stepping forward, Redon helped Calamity to her feet, keeping a hand on her arm and steadying her. Something of the old Calamity grin came to her face as she watched Jacqueline rise and saw the worried expressions on the two policemen's faces.

"Danged if that coloured water we've been drinking wasn't stronger'n I thought," she said. "It's sure rough on a lil country gal like me, that's not used to drinking it."

"It sure is," grinned the second policeman. "Why, anybody'd think you'd fainted had they seen you."

More feet approached, but again it proved to be friends who arrived. Redon nodded to the remainder of the escort as they came up.

"You got him!" one said.

"Yeah. Did the noise attract any attention?"

"None as we noticed, Raoul," the other policeman replied and glanced at the groaning man on the ground. "Did he say anything, Calam?"

"Let us not stand discussing it," Redon put in before Calamity could reply. "Let's get this feller to the station house. If folks hear we've nailed the Strangler, we'll have bad trouble on our hands. Feelings are high about him."

"You're right about that," Calamity agreed. "I saw a lynch mob one time in Butte. It grew from nothing to—well, I don't never want to see another."

She did not mention that the lynching was prevented by prompt action taken by a bunch of really efficient lawmen, but doubted if the New Orleans police would have the equipment or ability to halt a mob. Sure St. Andre and his boys were tough and real handy in their own way, but it took gun-skill to handle a mob filled with hate and the desire to shed the blood of a killer.

"Are you sure he didn't hurt you, Calam?" asked Jacqueline gently.

"Not as much as you did last night, gal."

"You didn't give him enough time," remarked Redon dryly. "Get him on his feet. The Chief of Police'll be pleased to see the Strangler."

"If it's the Strangler we caught," said Calamity.

All eyes turned first to Calamity, then swung in the direction of the groaning man on the ground. One of the escort swung back to face Calamity and nodded to her as she reached up to touch her throat with delicate fingers.

"How'd you mean, Calamity?" the man asked. "This feller tried to strangle you, didn't he?"

"Sure he did. With his bare hands," she answered. "Way I heard it, the others were all killed with a rope."

"Maybe he didn't have the cord with him tonight," Redon suggested.

"Could b—," began Calamity, then stopped talking as her range-trained ears caught some sounds the others missed. "Quick, somebody's coming. Get him on his feet and hid among you. Then make like you're all drunk."

Without arguing or wasting time, two of Redon's men grabbed the groaning Cope and hoisted him to his feet. Calamity, Jacqueline and the remaining pair of detectives bunched around Cope, hiding him from view. Two men and two street-girls came into sight, walking arm in arm along the path.

"Poor ole Charlie," Calamity said, in a fair impersonation of a whisky-loaded voice. "Reckon that last drink was too much for him."

"We'd best get him home," Redon answered, sounding just as convincing. "He sure sounds awful."

Suddenly Cope recovered enough to stop groaning and begin struggling, letting out a mouthful of curses and trying to free himself from the handcuffs. The detectives gripped his arms, but could do little or nothing about his voice. However, they did not need to worry about the passing party interfering. Taking a look

94

at the apparently drunken group, one of the street-girls gave a warning.

"The law'll be here soon. Let's get going."

Having no wish to be involved with the police, the girls' escorts hurried them by the swaying, rowdy group and along a path. Not one of the quartet realised they passed a group of law enforcement officers and a prisoner—perhaps even the Strangler himself—but took the others as being drunks liable to attract the attention of the police. Without a backward glance, the party hurried off and Redon stepped clear of his men, letting out a sigh and wiping his brow.

"All right," he said. "Let's get out of here. This'll make me old afore my time."

Keeping around Cope so as to prevent the fact that he wore handcuffs showing, the policemen started to walk him along the path towards the Latour Street entrance to City Park. Calamity and Jacqueline went along, adding their voices to the drunken song raised by the men to drown the struggling, raving Cope's tones.

"If he keeps this up, he'll bring the patrolman on the beat down on us," Redon remarked. "I'll have to quieten him."

"Do it easy," Calamity replied. "I'm still not sure we got the right man."

"Know something, Calam," Redon answered. "Neither am I."

On reaching the edge of the Park, Cope quietened down. Sending one of the men to find a couple of cabs, Redon kept the others in a group around their prisoner. Rowdy parties had never been so rare around the Latour Street district that they attracted any attention. Even the passing beat patrolmen gave the group no more than a glance before continuing on his way.

"We'll go straight to Headquarters," Redon decided when the cabs arrived. "You girls go in the second cab with Pete, the rest of us'll take Cope in the first. I won't be sorry to get him clear of here."

"What was it like, Calam?" Jacqueline asked as they sat in the cab and were carried towards the Police Headquarters.

"Bad, real bad!" Calamity answered and reached for the dancer's hands. "Let me handle it alone, Jackie gal."

"No!"

"Know something, you awkward little cuss. That's just what I thought you'd say. Only we'll have to make sure the boys get there quicker next time."

"Next time?" Jackie gasped. "But I thought—."

"I don't. This whole thing sits wrong with me," Calamity interrupted. "If he *is* the Strangler, why'd he change the way he killed? And why'd he chance making so much noise?"

On arrival at Headquarters, St. Andre expressed the same sentiments. Cope had sunk into sullen silence and steadfastly refused to answer any questions.

"Take him downstairs and keep him by himself," St. Andre ordered. "Then go to the riverfront and ask around the ocean-going ships, see if you can find where he came from."

The interview had been held in the Captain of Detective's office and St. Andre returned to his own room where Calamity and Jacqueline sat waiting for him.

"I think you're right, Calam," he said, his voice showing disappointment. "He's not the Strangler."

"Do you want us to try again tonight?" Calamity asked.

"No."

"We'll be out tomorrow then. And don't trying arguing, me 'n' Jackie here've made up our minds."

"All right. Tomorrow night then. Only this time I'll make sure the escort—."

"The boys did their best," Calamity interrupted. "Let's go, Jackie."

St. Andre escorted the girls to the front entrance of the building. After handing Jacqueline into the waiting cab, he turned to Calamity and took her hands in his.

"You took a risk. I don't know how I can ever thank you, *cherie*."

"Just come 'round to my place some time and we'll call each other liars," Calamity replied. "Goodnight, Sherry. Maybe we'll have better luck next time."

# CHAPTER ELEVEN

*Miss Canary Learns How It Is Done*

CALAMITY attracted some considerable interest when she strolled into the Police Headquarters building on the morning after the attempt on her life. The usual bunch of loungers in the main hall cast glances in her direction, for none of them were used to seeing a young woman dressed in trousers—especially tight-fitting pants such as Calamity wore. One of the girl's escort from the previous night came from where he had been sitting and nodded a greeting to her, then led her upstairs.

"Who's that?" asked one of the men to the desk sergeant.

"One of St. Andre's," the sergeant answered. "Not as fancy as some who've come to see him, but I bet she'd be a whole heap more woman."

Even had he wished to, the desk sergeant could not have given out the true reason for Calamity's visit. St. Andre insisted that only the people directly involved with the decoy job knew about it, for he did not wish word of his plan to leak out. Luckily for the scheme, young ladies visiting the handsome detective lieutenant had become common enough a sight not to attract any attention around Headquarters.

From the expression on her escort's face, Calamity guessed that their work of the previous night had not been entirely crowned with success. However, there were too many people on the stairs for a detailed discussion of the matter and Calamity reached the door of St. Andre's office knowing no more than when she entered the building. She knocked on the door, opened it and entered, coming to a halt as she saw St. Andre had a visitor.

"Sorry, Sh—Lootenant," she said. "They didn't say you had company."

"That's all right, Calam," St. Andre answered. "Come on in. This's Captain Holgate of the *China Star*. Captain, this is Miss Canary, the young woman who helped capture Cope last night."

Calamity looked at Holgate. A peaked hat sat on the man's head, his face had a weather-beaten look about it and bore an air of command. He wore a blue broadcloth uniform jacket of a kind

Calamity had never seen before, white trousers and well-polished boots. In height Holgate would almost equal Dobe Killem, though not quite so heavily built. Calamity took a liking to the man on sight, figuring he would be a good friend, but a real bad enemy.

"Howdy, Cap'n," she greeted, then looked at St. Andre. "Is Cope the Strangler, Sherry?"

"No," replied St. Andre, his voice bitter.

"Got to figuring that after he grabbed me," the girl admitted, walking forward and perching herself on the edge of St. Andre's desk. "He made too much noise and didn't use that cord."

"He also only docked late yesterday afternoon after a two year trip on the *China Star*," St. Andre went on, accepting a cigar from the case Holgate held out. "I wish it had been Cope. At least we would have the Strangler under lock and key now. But Cope hasn't been in this country for two years."

"Which same couldn't't've been him that killed the other girls then," Calamity remarked. "But why in hell did he jump me last night?"

"I can answer that, Miss—," Holgate said.

"Make it Calam, like everybody does," the girl told him, eyeing the cigar case as its owner extracted a weed and hoping he would offer her one.

Captain Holgate proved irresponsive to thought suggestions, for he did not catch Calamity's mental message and hand over his case for her to accept a cigar. Taking his seat, from which he rose when Calamity entered, the captain lit his cigar and looked at the girl through the smoke. Suddenly recalling his manners, he gave a guilty start and looked down at the smoking cigar between his fingers.

"I'm sorry, Miss—Calam—," he said. "Does the smoke bother you?"

"Only when I'm the only one not doing it," she answered.

With a grin, and a knowing wink at St. Andre, Holgate passed his cigar-case to the girl. His entire attitude was one of male superiority as he prepared to call Calamity's bluff. Knowing her better, St. Andre could have warned Holgate that any bluff Calamity put out was likely to be forced through to the end. Much to Holgate's surprise, Calamity took a cigar from the case, bit off its tip in a professional manner, accepted the light the detective offered her and proceeded to draw smoke from the rolled tobacco with evident enjoyment.

"What was you saying about that feller Cope, Cap'n?" she

asked calmly, ignoring St. Andre's broad grin and Holgate's bug-eyed stare.

"Who—Oh yes. Cope!" The words bounced out of the captain in disjointed flow as he wondered what kind of a woman sat before him. "He's one of my hands. A good worker until the trouble. You see, he married in New York and while he was away on a ship his wife became friendly with a girl called Mavis. Apparently this Mavis was a bad one and she steered Cope's wife astray. When Cope came in from the voyage, he found he no longer had a home and his wife had gone. He met her later, working in a waterfront hell on the New York docks. When he got the story out of her, he went hunting for Mavis. New York's a big city and he never found her. After a time he went back to sea. The trouble was that when he came to port and took a few drinks, he went looking for Mavis. No matter where the ship happened to be, he looked for her. Twice he was jailed for attacking blonde girls, but was fined and released."

"And you kept him on, knowing that?" Calamity said.

"He was a good sailor and they're hard to find. I thought it was just a drunken brawl and never troubled to go too deeply into the matter. On board he never made any trouble. Then last night, when the police came asking about him, I found two of his ship-mates and got the full story out of them. Apparently he had been brooding about his wife for days and gave them the slip when he went ashore. He must have gone looking for that girl Mavis and picked on you—but why you I don't know. Mavis was a blonde."

"So was I last night," Calamity replied. "I feel sorta sorry for him. What'll happen to him, Sherry?"

"We'll have to take him to trial," the detective answered.

"But if the Cap'n here takes him—."

"No, cherie. The next time he gets ashore and looks for Mavis, the girl he finds won't have a police escort—or be Calamity Jane."

"I'm afraid Lieutenant St. Andre is right, Calam," Holgate went on.

"By the way, Calam, the captain had seen the Strangler's last victim and thinks he knows how the killing is done."

"It's hardly a thing to tell a lady," Holgate objected.

"Ain't no ladies here that I know of," Calamity remarked, sucking appreciatively at the cigar. "This's a right good smoke, cap'n. How'd he do the killing?"

Holgate did not answer immediately. Looking at the girl, he suddenly became aware that she did not try to prove anything, but really enjoyed the cigar. Here was a girl completely beyond his knowledge of women, one who lived by her own rules and neither accepted favours because of her sex, nor tried to out-do men despite it. He decided he could talk to Calamity with the same freedom that he discussed matters with his ship's officers.

"It's an old Indian trick," he explained. "One of my crew was killed in Bombay by the *thuggi*, they're a religious cult who dabble in murder and robbery. The way the *thuggi* kill is with a cord slipped around the victim's throat in a special manner. It is silent, quick and gives the victim little or no chance of escape or countering the hold. From the marks on the dead girl's neck, I'd say the Strangler either knows about the *thuggi*, or has come up with a mighty close imitation of their methods."

"What the hell's tribe do these *thuggi* belong to?" asked Calamity. "It don't sound Cheyenne, Sioux or Comanche to me, nor any of the tamed tribes neither. And I never heard of no place called Bombay on the Great Plains."

"That's not surprising," smiled Holgate. "Bombay is in India, and the *thuggi* are real Indians, not the kind you're used to meeting."

"Cap'n," grunted Calamity. "Happen you saw a bunch of them red varmints on the warpath, you'd reckon they was real enough."

"The captain offered to show us how *thuggi* works, Calam," St. Andre remarked with a smile, wondering if he would ever cease to be amused by the girl's unique female outlook on life.

"Yeah," replied Calamity suspiciously, putting a hand to her throat. "And who's he going to do the showing on?"

"On me, of course," the detective answered. "Who else?"

"Just thought you might want to see it done on me, just so's you'd know how it was done. Seeing it's you who gets it, Sherry, let's take us a whirl."

Reaching into his jacket pocket, Holgate took out a length of stout whipcord. Doubling the cord to find its centre, Holgate tied a knot in the middle, then one more on either side and about three inches from the first. With the knots tied, Holgate gripped the cord at each end, allowing it to hang in a long loop before him.

"Ready, lieutenant?" he asked.

Standing up with his back to Holgate, St. Andre nodded. "Ready!"

Holgate stepped forward and flipped the loop over St. Andre's head, gripped both ends of the cord between his hands and pivoted so that he stood back to back with the detective. Now the cord passed from Holgate's hands, up over his right shoulder and around St. Andre's neck. Bending forward, Holgate drew the loop tight. Only for an instant did Holgate keep up the tension, but St. Andre felt the knots bite into the sides and centre of his throat, blocking the windpipe and stopping his breath.

"That's how they do it," Holgate said, releasing the cord and turning fast. "Are you all right, lieutenant?"

Jerking the cord hurriedly from his throat, St. Andre sucked in a deep breath before he nodded and replied, "I—I think so. Do you know of any way one can break the grip of the cord, Captain?"

"None. The *thuggi* always tries to take his victim by surprise. Once the noose falls and is drawn tight, there is no escape."

"That's what I thought," St. Andre said quietly and turned to Calamity. "I've decided—."

"And so have I!" Calamity interrupted. "I'm still going through with it. So you'd best try that trick on me, Cap'n, and let me get the feel of it."

"On *you?*" gasped Holgate.

"On me. I'm the one the Strangler'll be doing it on."

Throwing an appealing glance at St. Andre, Holgate hoped for moral support in his refusal; but did not get it.

"When Calamity makes up her mind, we poor men might just as well give up and let her have her way," the detective stated. "She's seen enough to know how to make a *thuggi* cord, and she's stubborn enough to find help in practicing escaping from it. So we might as well help her."

"You might just as well," agreed Calamity, laying her cigar in the ashtray on St. Andre's desk.

Coming to her feet, Calamity stepped forward and took St. Andre's place before Holgate. After throwing another imploring glance at St. Andre, the captain took up his cord and stepped into position behind the girl. Calamity waited, tense and ready, watching for the cord to pass before her eyes. While watching the demonstration on St. Andre, she had seen what might be a way of breaking the hold and wanted to try it.

Down came the noose and instantly Calamity brought up her hands, palms outwards, sliding her fingers under the cord in an attempt at stopping it drawing tight on her. The try failed miserably. She felt the cord jerk tight as Holgate turned, and the leverage slammed her hands back into her throat, the knuckles sinking into her flesh. A sudden feeling of panic hit the girl at the way her breath was chopped off and she tried to jerk forward; which only made the grip on her throat tighten. Then the cord slackened and she staggered forward, tearing it from her neck.

St. Andre sprang forward and caught the girl in his arms, while Holgate spung around, concern showing plain on his face.

"Are you all right, *cherie*?" asked St. Andre, for he had seen the momentary panic on her face.

"Did I hurt you?" Holgate went on before Calamity could reply.

The concern for her welfare shown by St. Andre and Holgate jolted Calamity back to her normal self and she managed a weak grin.

"Yes for you, Sherry, and no to the Cap'n. Only I know one way I *can't* chance using now."

Yet while she fought to hide it, Calamity felt very worried. Holgate had moved slowly and with care, she had been ready and waiting for the noose too, yet he still managed to snap her hands back against her throat and prevent her from pulling the cord even a little free. Of course the leverage on the cord as it passed over Holgate's shoulder accounted for the strength of its grip, but the same would apply just as much when the Strangler wielded the noose. Another point to be remembered was that the Strangler would move neither as slowly nor gently as did Holgate when applying his killing cord.

Never one to avoid facing the truth, Calamity reviewed the situation in the light of what she now knew. One thing stood out clear and simple. If she hoped to stay alive long enough for the protective police screen to arrive and save her, she must find some way of breaking the hold of the cord around her neck. There now only remained one problem to be solved, the most important matter of all—how to do the breaking.

Taking off her bandana, Calamity spread it out flat, then folded it lengthways instead of re-rolling it. Carefully she wrapped the bandana around her neck to act as some slight protection against the cut of the cord. Giving a weak grin, she looked at the two men.

"Try again, Cap—Nope, you'd best let Sherry handle the rope this time, 'cause I'm going to try like hell to get free, and he's paid to take the lumps."

"Thank you for your concern, *cherie*," said the detective. "But let the Captain do it once more while I watch. I may be able to see some way of breaking the hold while watching."

On the first attempt, Calamity tried lashing with her right foot. She missed her mark, lost her balance and only the fact that Holgate instantly released the cord saved Calamity from obtaining a too thorough idea of how the cord worked. Without her hands on the cord, Calamity learned the purpose of the three knots. The lump of the central knot pressed on her adam's apple, the other two closing in from the sides so as to effectively clamp shut her wind-pipe. Even through the folds of the bandana she could feel the pressure of the knots, and guessed at the sensation caused when they bit into naked flesh.

A shudder ran through Calamity as the noose slackened, but she fought down her fears. Thinking fast, she came up with a possible solution.

"Kicking won't work," she said. "Try again."

On the next try Calamity made an attempt at stepping to one side. She hoped to pull the cord from Holgate's shoulder. However, she made a mistake by stepping to her right and this only drew the cord tighter.

"That won't work," St. Andre warned as the cord slackened.

"I kinda figured that myself," admitted Calamity.

"Try stepping to your left next time. It might pull the cords off his shoulder."

"Let me catch my breath first. Then we'll try it your way, Sherry."

An expression of admiration came to Holgate's face as he coiled the cord and watched Calamity pick up her cigar.

"If you don't mind me saying so, Calamity," he said. "You're the bravest woman I've ever seen or met."

"Feel free to say it any time," she replied, hoping she was not blushing at the praise. "Only I'm not being brave. I'm just a half-smart lil country gal trying to act all smart and save her fool neck."

"If you're a *half*-smart country girl," St. Andre put in, "I'd hate to come across a smart one."

"Or I," Holgate went on. "Any time you need a job, come and see me. I could use you as mate on my ship."

"Let's make another stab at escaping," Calamity put in hurriedly and knew she *was* blushing now.

Even stepping to the left did not provide the necessary solution to the problem, for the cord would not slide off of Holgate's shoulder and only drew tighter. Calamity let out an exasperated snort when released.

"Say, do you have that itty-bitty stingy gun with you, Sherry?" she asked.

"Of course," St. Andre answered, taking out his Smith & Wesson.

"Unload it. Let's try something else. Maybe if I'd a gun in my reticule, I could get it out and use it."

"It's worth a try," the detective admitted. "I've got the dead girl's reticule in my desk, seeing that you didn't bring one along."

"It don't go with pants and a shirt," explained the fashion-conscious Miss Canary and looked at Holgate. "You'll have to hold the cord a mite longer this time."

After St. Andre unloaded his revolver, he took the reticule from the desk's drawer, handing weapon and bag to the girl. Calamity double-checked on the empty condition of the gun, a safety precaution St. Andre approved of, then placed the revolver into the bag and drew tight the draw-strings which closed the neck of the reticule.

"Let's go," she said, standing with the reticule swinging by its strings from her left wrist.

Once more the noose dropped into place and even as it did, Calamity grabbed for the reticule with her right hand. She tried to move fast, but not fumble, yet for all that she barely slid her hand into the reticule before the cord around her throat drew tight. She found that the sudden cutting off of her breath, even though she expected it, induced a state of near-panic which prevented her thinking. Desperately she began to struggle against the choking of the cord.

"Let loose!" St. Andre yelled.

Holgate obeyed instantly and Calamity sank to her knees, hands jerking the cord and bandana from her throat. Both men moved to her side and gentle hands lifted her to a chair. The roaring in her head subsided and she saw two worried faces before her.

"That's all, *cherie*," St. Andre announced grimly.

"I just didn't move fast enough," she objected.

"And the Strangler will be moving much faster than I did," Holgate pointed out. "Surely there's some other way. Can't your men stick closer to her?"

"Not as close as they'd have to be to make it safe, or the Strangler would see them, especially in the Park."

"How well can Raoul Redon and the other boys shoot?" asked Calamity.

"Fairly well," answered St. Andre.

"Well enough to pick the Strangler off me from thirty yards at least on a moonlight night?"

"*Sacre blue!*" gasped the detective. "I doubt it. Hey, how about one of your friends with the freight outfit?"

For a moment loyalty to her friends warred with common sense and in the end common sense won. While Calamity hated to admit it, she doubted if even Dobe Killem could handle a revolver that well. A rifle maybe; but one did not see folks walking around in New Orleans with a rifle tucked under an arm. To have one of the boys do so would attract too much attention.

"None of 'em could do it. There's none of the boys can handle a gun that good."

"Or my men," St. Andre admitted.

"It's a pity you don't have one of those Western gunfighters here," Holgate remarked.

"Somebody like Dusty Fog, you m—."

St. Andre's sentence never ended. Giving a whoop like a drunk Pawnee coming to a pow wow, Calamity sprang forward, grabbed him by the shoulders and gave him a resounding kiss.

"That's it, Sherry!" she whooped. "If there's any way of getting out of the cord, old Dusty'll be the one to know it."

"Dusty Fog is not in New Orleans," St. Andre pointed out.

"Some detective," sniffed Calamity. "Don't they have a telegraph office in this fancy big city?"

"It's a chance," St. Andre admitted. "Captain Fog knows that strange way of fighting. He might be able to come up with the answer. We'll get off a message to him right away. But if he doesn't come up with the answer, we'll call off the whole thing."

# CHAPTER TWELVE

## *Miss Canary Attracts Attention*

ST. ANDRE turned to Calamity as they left the telegraph office after dispatching the request for advice to Dusty Fog in the Rio Hondo country of Texas.

"That is that, *cherie*," he said. "The answer will be sent over to my office as soon as it arrives."

"If Dusty's at the OD Connected, we'll get an answer right soon," Calamity replied. "What're you going to do now?"

"Make another tour of the Latour Street district and see if I can find anybody ready to talk about a missing girl. And you?"

"There's no use in my going with you. Happen the Strangler should see us together in daylight, he might be able to recognise me later, even through that blonde hair and paint."

"You could take up Captain Holgate's offer of a tour of inspection of the *China Star*," St. Andre suggested, for the captain had made the offer before leaving Headquarters to rejoin his ship.

"Sure I could. Might do that later. Only right now I've a hankering to see what kind of hosses the Army brought us down here to collect."

"Then I'll see you—."

"Tonight, same as last," Calamity finished for him. "We'll just have to play 'em as they fall until we get word from Dusty."

Seeing there was no chance of changing Calamity's mind, and knowing she would probably be stubborn enough to go without an escort, St. Andre surrendered. He hailed a passing cab and handed the girl into it, then gave the driver instructions where to take her.

"Until tonight then, *cherie*," St. Andre finished, taking the girl's hand and kissing it.

"Yep," agreed Calamity. "Hooray wah! Hey, what do you know, I talk French now."

Standing on the sidewalk, St. Andre watched the cab pull away. Maybe Miss Martha Jane Canary lacked most of the social graces, but there would never be another girl like her. With that thought St. Andre turned and looked for transportation to take him on what his instincts told him would be another dud quest to learn the identity of the Strangler's victims.

The cab carried Calamity towards the waterfront area. Cattle and other livestock came into New Orleans and an open section of the docks had been given over to pens. Leaving the cab, Calamity walked towards the largest of the pens and as she drew close, the wind wafted the smell of horses to her nostrils. Calamity sucked in the aroma as eagerly as a bluetick hound hitting hot cougar scent. In her imagination, she was carried back to her beloved West. Suddenly Calamity felt homesick for the rolling Great Plains country. She longed to feel leather in her hands as she handled the ribbons of her big Conestoga wagon's team, feel the sun on her head, the wind or rain in her face. The big city was not for Calamity Jane and never would be. She hated the never-ending rush and bustle of New Orleans, where folks hardly had time to stop and talk a spell. Out on the Great Plains everything seemed calmer, more friendly, cleaner. Even death came openly on the Plains, from bullet, arrow, knife or war-lance, not sneaking, unseen, silent and cowardly as the Strangler's whipcord noose.

"Now easy there, Calam gal," she told herself. "You've had some fun here too."

A young cavalry lieutenant, far more tidy and glittering than the junior officers Calamity had met on the Plains, stood by Dobe Killem's side at the largest of the coral-like pens. Turning from their study of the forty or so horses in the pen, both men looked in Calamity's direction and Killem raised his hand in greeting.

"Hi there, Calam gal," he said. "Come on up and get acquainted with Lootenant Bristow."

Trying not to stare too pointedly at Calamity's shapely figure and unorthodox dress style, Bristow bowed as taught at West Point.

"My pleasure, ma'am," he said.

"Reckon it is," grinned the girl and thrust out her right hand.

Hurriedly Bristow jerked off his right gauntlet and accepted the girl's hand. With the formalities tended to, Calamity turned and swung up on the pen's top rail to study the horses.

"What do you think of them, Miss Canary?" Bristow inquired.

"They look a mite small to me. Can't see one as goes fifteen hands even."

"We didn't buy them for great size, but for their hooves."

Ducking between the rails, Calamity entered the corral. Unlike Western horses, the animals in the pen showed no desire to avoid human beings, allowing Calamity to approach them. Although the girl had not worn her gunbelt that morning, the bull whip was thrust into her waist belt. Pulling the whip out, she made a loop of part of its lash and dropped it over the head of the nearest horse. Holding the animal, Calamity glanced down, then bent to take a closer look at its hooves.

Full of male superiority, Bristow joined Calamity in the pen and pointed down at what interested the girl.

"That's why the Army bought these horses," he explained. "They're called muck-ponies and bred between here and Florida. See the sizes of the hooves?"

"I'd be hard put not to."

"Despite the size, the foot is light, yet, tough," Bristow went on, lifting the horse's near fore leg to emphasise his point. "See the small size of the frog? It leaves a deep hollow into which mud can pack tight enough to support the horse's weight when crossing ground into which an animal with a normal hoof would sink belly deep. Why, I've seen muck ponies canter across swampy ground and quicksands that would mire down any other horse, and carrying weight too."

"That'd be real useful," answered Calamity, "in swampy country. Only we're a mite long on swamps on the Great Plains."

"You have snow there."

"Yep, reckon we do. It gets real de—Hey, you mean that the army figures using these hosses for a winter campaign again the Injuns?"

"Something like that," Bristow agreed. "You know as well as I do that the campaign against the Indians is almost brought to a halt with the snows of winter?"

"Reckon it is," the girl admitted, releasing the horse.

"We hope the muck ponies will enable us to carry on the offensive through the winter. That's why we bought them."

"Now me," grinned Calamity, "I thought that some general'd bred too many hosses and wanted to sell 'em fast."

Bristow eyed Calamity coldly and stiffened slightly, for he was still fresh enough from West Point to take himself and life very seriously. Before he could think up a sufficiently chilling response to her remark, he saw something which made him let the matter slide. A two-horse carriage driven by a grizzled infantry sergeant approached, in it sat a tall, slim major-general, a plump, motherly-looking woman and a pretty girl dressed to the height of fashion.

"Excuse me, Miss Canary," Bristow said stiffly, then turned and left the pen. Watching him go, Calamity coiled her whip and thrust it into her waist band. "Damn fool gal!" she told herself. "That big mouth of your'n'll get you hung one of these days."

Following Bristow from the corral, Calamity leaned on the rail and watched the young officer march smartly to the carriage and throw a parade-ground salute to the general.

"At ease, Douglas," the general said. "We came down to see that horse I had shipped in for Aileen's birthday."

"Mr. Killem cut it out for me, sir. I had it put in the smaller, empty pen."

"Good horse?"

"A fine animal, sir, but a touch high spirited."

"How about the others, Dobe?" asked the general, turning to the freighter.

"I've looked 'em over, General," Killem replied. "They're in good shape. I reckon we'll still have some alive when we reach St. Jo."

"They'd better be, or I'll be coming to you for employment," grinned General Furlong. "This idea is costing money and Congress hates spending *that* on the Army in times of peace."

"Reckon those muck-ponies'll do what you want?" asked Calamity.

"I hope so. The main idea came from Sheridan, I believe. If the ponies can take the cold, they might help us hit at the Indians during winter."

"May we see my new horse, papa?" Aileen Furlong asked.

"That's what we're here for," the General replied.

Although nobody asked her, Calamity accompanied Furlong's party to one of the other pens. Hooking a foot on to the bottom rail, Calamity studied the fifteen hand black gelding inside. She liked what she saw and to her way of thinking there stood a tolerable piece of horse-flesh, dainty, shapely, proud and spirited. The kind of animal one would pick as a go-to-town horse, yet capable of doing a hard day's work.

"He's a beauty, papa," Aileen gasped. "May I try him?"

"You're hardly dressed for riding, dear," her mother put in.

"And the horse is too much for a woman yet, Aileen," Bristow went on. "It needs gentling before you use it."

"Nonsense!" Aileen snorted. "I've been riding—."

"I'd rather see the horse ridden before we make any decisions," interrupted Furlong. "I'd ask you if you weren't in uniform, Douglas. How about it, Dobe?"

At which point Calamity put her bill in. While not setting up as a militant feminist who believed she could do anything a man could and better, Calamity took a dim view of Furlong and Bristow's display of arrogant male superiority. And with Miss

Martha Jane Canary to take a dim view of anything was to act in an attempt to clear her vision.

"Hell, Dobe totes too much lard to ride a hoss that size," she said. "I'll go in and 'three-saddle' it for you."

All eyes turned to the girl and grins creased the faces of the two older men, although Bristow clearly did not approve of Calamity's free and easy attitude. Having been on the Great Plains with her husband, Mrs. Furlong had lost any snobbish ideas of class-distinction she once possessed, so she smiled at the Western girl's speech. Aileen was young enough to regard Calamity as daring, modern and unconventional—in which she did Calamity an injustice—so must also be someone to respect.

"I could have one of the regimental horse-masters take it in hand, sir," Bristow suggested.

"And they'd spoil it for the gal," Calamity sniffed. "They're all right for busting a hoss so some lead-butted recruit can sit it, but that black wants gentler handling."

While General Furlong would not openly admit it, he knew army trainers were of necessity often heavy-handed in their training methods and tended to break rather than gentle a horse. Such treatment would ruin the black for his daughter's use. Anyway, it might be fun to see if Calamity Jane stacked up as high as Dobe Killem claimed for her.

"Do you have a saddle here?" he asked.

"The boys rode down this morning, their rigs are hanging on the rail at the big pen," answered Calamity. "Happen Mr. Killem'll act like a lil gentleman and fetch one over for me, I'll go catch me a hoss."

"I'll tend to it," grinned Killem.

Swinging into the pen, Calamity walked across the hard-packed ground towards the horse. However, the black did not wish to be caught and had room in which to manoeuvre. Showing a neat use of speed and the ability to turn on a dime, the horse refused to be caught for a time. This made Calamity use some choice language not often heard on the lips of a young lady and caused Aileen to jerk up her fan to hide her smile. A small crowd of loafers, the kind of men who gathered everywhere when given a chance of watching other people work, stood around the pen and sniggers sounded.

"All right!" Calamity snorted, coming to a halt and eyeing the horse. "If that's how want it."

Drawing her bull whip free, she shook out the lash then sent it snaking through the air to coil around the black's neck. Outside the pen Aileen gave a little shriek of dismay, while Bristow gave an angry snort aimed to let folks know his lack of faith in Calamity had been justified. General Furlong, a man with some knowledge of horses, noted that the black did not scream or show any sign of pain as the whip landed.

"Ooh!" gasped Aileen. "Did you see that?"

"It's—," her father began.

Before the General could say more, Calamity raised her voice in a lady-like plea for assistance.

"Dobe! You and that shavetail shove your tired butt-ends over here and lend me a hand to toss leather on this fool critter!"

"Be right there, gal," Killem chorused back and held the saddle he carried in Bristow's direction. "Here, bring this in. I'll toss a rope on that black."

From the quiet manner in which the horse stood after feeling the whip's lash coil around its neck, Calamity decided it had been rope-broke at least. However, her whip could not hope to equal a sixty foot length of hard-plaited manila rope when it came to holding a horse, so she raised no objections when Killem joined her and dabbed a loop on the black's neck. Calamity shook free, coiled and belted the whip. Clearly the horse did not intend to stand mildly and have the saddle fixed on it. In fact the black kicked up quite a commotion and attracted more loafers to see the fun.

"We'll have to ear him down," Killem stated, bracing himself against the pull of the horse and watching Calamity and Bristow's tries at getting the saddle in position.

"I'll tend to it!" whooped Calamity.

Watching her chance, the girl darted forward and grabbed to catch the rearing black by one ear. Making her catch, she reached around, took hold of the other ear and used her weight to get the black on to all four feet again. Calamity felt the horse strain against her grasp and as a further inducement to good behaviour took hold of the tip of the nearest ear between her teeth. Apparently the horse knew what Calamity's action meant, for it stopped struggling and avoided taking further pain. For all his smart and pompous manner, Bristow moved fast. Although he was more used to the Army's McClennan saddle, he wasted no time in swinging the range rig into place and securing it on the black.

While this went on, Tophet Tombes had returned from checking on the flatboats in which the horses would be transported north. He was on the opposite side of the corral to Furlong's party, but leaned on the rail among the loafers to watch the fun. A trio of burly, hard-looking men stood close by him. Brutal and coarse though they looked, all wore better clothing than the crowd around them. The tallest of the party had a livid weal running from the right temple across to below the lobe of his left ear. Nor were his friends clean of face, for one sported a swollen, cut lip and black eye, while the other's nose looked enlarged from some recent damage. Tombes noticed none of this, being more interested in watching the saddling of the black and awaiting Calamity showing those city folks a thing or two about the art of horse-handling Western style.

Never one to disappoint an audience, Calamity fixed herself to give the onlookers a good show. First she checked that the horse's saddle sat just as she wanted it, then fitted the bridle in place and cast off Killem's rope. Gripping the saddlehorn and reins, Calamity went afork the horse in a lithe bound.

"Yeeagh!" she yelled and rammed both heels into the horse's ribs, causing Killem and Bristow to make hurried dives towards the pen's rails.

It took but three bucking jumps to tell Calamity that the horse had already been 'three-saddled', ridden by a buster the three times which were all considered necessary out West for the horse to be ready to hand on to its regular owner. However, the black proved to be a show bucker, tucking its nose between its front legs, arching its back and going high but straight forward. While such a style looked highly spectacular, especially to an audience who saw few such sights, it was not difficult for a skilled rider to handle. Calamity knew that as long as she did not fall asleep, she could stay afork the black and would not wind up eating pen-dirt without stooping for it.

Not that Calamity was content merely to take the conceit and bed-springs out of the black's belly in solid chunks. To whet the appetites of the crowd, she pretended to be losing her seat, waving as if off balance. A yell of applause rose as she fought her way back into control.

"Dang that Calamity," grinned Killem. "She'll bust her fool neck one of these fine days."

"I've never seen such a splendid rider," Aileen breathed back.

"Likely," grunted the big freighter, for he knew a show bucker when he saw one. "Stay with it, Calam gal!"

However, the horse decided to call it a day. Having been 'three-saddled', the black horse knew better than fight against the inevitable, and its snuffy nature sprang more from not being worked recently than out of a bad spirit. So, finding its rider clearly intended to stay afork, the black stopped fighting. Calamity fanned the horse's ears with her hat and jabbed moccasined heels into its ribs, but to no avail. Never one to punish a horse for showing a little spirit, she rode the black to the side of the pen and dropped from the saddle.

"There you are," she said to Aileen. "You've got a good hoss here, gal."

"I'll walk him until he cools, Aileen," Bristow put in and swung into the pen to take the black's reins from Calamity.

"Thank you for riding the horse, Miss—," Aileen began.

"Never been one for 'Missing', unless I don't like the other gal," Calamity interrupted. "Call me Calam."

"Thank you, Calamity," smiled Aileen. "I thought when you used the whip—."

Aileen's words trailed off again, for she did not know how to express her fears and wondered if Calamity might take offence at criticism.

Standing at Aileen's side, Killem let out a bellow of laughter. "The hoss wouldn't get hurt, unless Calam meant it to."

"But how could she—?" Mrs. Furlong put in.

Seeing that Aileen also appeared to have doubts about her ability to handle the whip, Calamity decided to demonstrate and prove her employer's words. The fact that a good-sized crowd also stood watching did not worry Calamity in the least, for she had never been a blushing violet seeking to hide her talents.

"Toss me my whip, Dobe," she said.

A grin creased Killem's face as he complied with his employee's request. Being a member of the bull-whip breed himself, Killem liked to see an expert at the art in action; and despite her age and sex Calamity was about as expert as one could be in the handling of a long lashed bull whip.

Catching the whip Killem tossed to her, Calamity shook out its coils and prepared to show the watching crowd how a Western freighter handled his, or her, most valued possession. The whip she held had been specially made for her by Tophet Tombes, who had a reputation for being something of an authority on such matters. Made of finest leather, the twenty foot lash was lighter than usual, yet that made the whip no less effective, handy—and deadly—in Calamity's skilled hands.

While knowing she was attracting considerable attention to herself and her unusual—for a female—talents, Calamity did not guess just what result her forthcoming demonstration of the ancient art of whip-popping would have.

# CHAPTER THIRTEEN

*Miss Canary Renews An Acquaintance*

As a starter to her display Calamity worked the whip back and forward in the air so its tip gave out a series of cracks like a volley of gun shots. This in itself was not a particularly difficult trick, but always made an impressive commencement to a demonstration of the whip-wielder's art. While cracking the whip, Calamity pondered on which of her extensive repertoire would be best to use as opener to her show. She wanted something spectacular, yet which could be topped by a climax at her completion of the demonstration.

General Furlong remembering a trick performed by an Army wagon master and whip expert, took the matter of selection from Calamity's hands. Taking a silver dollar from his pants pocket, Furlong tossed the coin so it landed at Calamity's feet. Calamity grinned, guessed at the trick required by Furlong and accepted the challenge. Stepping over the coin, she advanced seven paces towards the centre of the pen and the crowd watched in silence, wondering what she planned to do. Calamity turned, sending the whip's lash snaking out the moment she faced where the coin lay. An explosive crack sounded, a spurt of dust rose from the hard-packed ground, and the coin spun high into the air. Having duplicated the Army expert's trick, Calamity next proceeded to improve on it. Striding forward, she caught the coin as it fell and flipped it back to its owner.

Never one to miss being in on any fun going, Tophet Tombes finished rolling a cigarette. Gripping the top rail of the pen, he swung himself up and sat astride the pole.

"Got a light, Calam?" he yelled and thrust the cigarette between his teeth.

Turning to face the speaker, Calamity saw an opening for a more spectacular trick. Without ever having been on a stage, or in a business that required a study of human nature, Calamity knew instinctively that her next trick would go down better if she showed folks just how dangerous it could be.

Instead of striking at the cigarette jutting from Tombes' mouth, Calamity aimed slightly ahead of the scout and let her lash coil around the rail on which he sat. Excited and unbelieving comments rose as the nearest of the audience saw the groove Calamity's whip carved in the stout timber. Having duly impressed her audience, Calamity went ahead with the trick.

Taking sight carefully, for a wrong move could be deadly, Calamity struck again. Crack! The whip made its noise and the cigarette in Tombes' mouth burst into a ruined cloud of paper and shreds of tobacco. Mutters and chatter rose as the watching crowd realised that Calamity had shattered the cigarette without also carving a sizeable divot out of the scout's face.

"I still think that whip hurt my horse!" Aileen stated as Calamity began another series of whip cracks.

"Do, huh?" grunted Killem. "Watch this."

Swinging up on the pen's rail, Killem rolled back his shirt's left sleeve and extended a brawny, bare arm shoulder high. Calamity nodded and moved closer. Once more she sent the whip licking out, its tip kicking a chip of wood from the rail and hacking a gouge in the timber. Drawing back her arm again, Calamity took careful sight and estimated the distance. Out coiled the long lash, headed straight at Dobe Killem's bared arm.

Aileen gasped and tried to look away. Even the river loafers, men with little or no interest in anything other than themselves, held their breath as the whip's lash, which had carved a groove in solid timber, curled itself around Killem's flesh. Yet Killem gave no sign of pain, his grin never flickered for an instant; and when the lash fell away Aileen could see no damage to the freighter's skin.

"But—But—!" she gasped.

"It's all in how you strike," Furlong told his daughter. "Used one way that whip would strip the flesh from a man's bones—."

"Charles!" yelped his wife.

"D—Don't, papa!" Aileen went on with a shudder.

"All right, honey. But used the other, and I doubt if Calamity would tell you how it's done, the whip just coils around and doesn't hurt."

Across the pen, Calamity's skin was attracting just as much attention, but for a different reason. The burly man with the livid weal on his face ran his forefinger along the groove left by the whip, then touched the ridge on his face. Twisting his face into what might be passed as a friendly grin, the man turned to Tombes.

"Who's that gal?"

"That's Calamity Jane, friend," Tombes replied, a touch of pride in his voice.

"Reckon you must know her real well, letting her take that cigarette out of your mouth," the man went on. "I sure as hell wouldn't want to chance it."

"There's no danger with a gal like Calamity handling the whip," Tombes answered.

"She's good with one, huh?" put in a second of the trio, fingering his side.

"As good as they come," Tombes stated.

The interest shown by the men did not strike Tombes as being strange. He knew that few city folks ever saw a member of the bull whip breed in action. Nor did the scout give a thought to the mark across the biggest man's cheek.

"I'd sure hate her to take into me with that damned thing," remarked the third man. "Don't reckon she would though."

"Wouldn't, huh?" grinned Tombes. "There's a bunch in town who don't reckon so."

"How's that?" asked the biggest man.

"Night we arrived ole Calam run across a bunch jumping a young feller and cut in to help him. Turned——."

"Hey, Tophet!" Calamity called. "Come on over and let's see what else we can show 'em."

"Why sure," Tombes replied and jumped down from the fence to walk over to where Calamity stood.

"Reckon it's her, Jules?" the second man asked, watching Tombes slouch away.

"She'd be the right size, and that damned thing sounded just like when whoever it was jumped us. Let's go tell Max about this."

"Danged lil show-off," grinned Tombes as he joined Calamity.

"Was just showing them how the other half live," she replied. "Anyways, I didn't want that gal thinking I'd hurt her hoss."

"Some fellers over that way was some took by you, gal," the scout remarked.

"Where they at?"

"Over there—Nope, that's them just walking away. Fact being, one of 'em looked like he might've tangled with a whip his-self."

Calamity stopped coiling her whip and looked in the direction indicated by the scout. Even as she looked, a fourth man joined the trio. A low hiss left Calamity's lips as she saw that the new-comer's right arm hung in a sling. The quartet stood for a moment, then began to walk away towards the waterfront.

"Go tell Dobe to come with you!" she ordered.

"Where to?" barked Tombes after the girl's departing back.

"After me!" Calamity answered over her shoulder and headed for the pen's rail, coiling her whip as she walked.

"Danged fool female!" snorted Tombes. "It's being in the city made her *loco*—or wuss'n she was afore."

Shaking his head, but also grinning as he thought of the many sterling qualities which sprang from Calamity's *'loco'* behaviour, Tombes crossed the pen and climbed out. However, before he could prevent his boss leaving and deliver Calamity's message, Tombes saw Killem and Furlong walk towards where Lieutenant Bristow returned from walking and cooling out the black horse.

"Where's Calam?" Killem asked when his scout arrived.

"Danged if I know," Tombes admitted. "Soon's as I told her about them three fellers, she took out like the devil after a yearling."

"Know the gal likes company," Killem remarked. "But them fellers must be real something happen *she* chases after *them*."

"And me," drawled the scout. "They wasn't none of 'em what anybody 'cepting maybe their mothers'd think worth looking at. One of 'em looked like he'd already tangled with a whip."

On the night Calamity told her friends of how she rescued St. Andre, Tombes had been drinking; which always affected his memory. However, Killem, more sober at the time, took in Calamity's story and could remember enough of it to understand her present interest in a man with what might be whip-marked features. Despite her wild nature, Calamity was not a promiscuous girl who threw herself at every man she met. If Calamity took out after three men, she did not do so for sexual reasons but because she suspected them of being part of the quartet which jumped St. Andre.

"That danged lil fool hot-head!" Killem spat out. "Let's get after her."

"What's wrong, Dobe?" Furlong asked, but the freighter and scout already strode away at a good speed.

"Our lil gal's likely to find herself with some bad trouble," Killem called back over his shoulder.

On leaving the corral, Calamity passed through a crowd of excited admirers, grinning and acknowledging their approbation but keeping an eye on the departing quartet. The loafers, seeing there would be no more free entertainment, separated to go about their business. Ignoring the men behind her, Calamity strode through the waterfront area following the four bulky shapes. As she walked, she hoped to see a policeman who she might take into her confidence. Not that Calamity reckoned she would need help, but merely wished to have some official on hand to take over if the four men should be the same who attacked St. Andre. Even as she walked, Calamity found herself wishing that she had flouted New Orleans' rules and worn her gunbelt that morning.

After walking for a short way, the four men turned into an area given over to stacking cotton bales ready for shipment. The bales stood in high rows, separated by lanes through which roustabouts could move and handle the cargo. Reaching the corner, Calamity turned it, looked along the lane. She could see no sign of the quartet along the hundred or more yards length before her, but there were numerous side paths down which they might have gone. Figuring this would be as good a time and place as any to get in closer, Calamity strode along the lane at a better pace.

A movement caught Calamity's eye as she passed one of the side lanes. Fast though her reactions were, Calamity left things just a shade too long. Even as she started to turn, right hand reaching for her whip, she saw the big tough with the livid weal on his face, and a second hard-looking cuss standing concealed by the bales. Out shot the bigger man's hand, gripping Calamity by the right shoulder, digging in and pulping it so she could not make the arm muscles work. With a heave, the man plucked Calamity into the lane and his companion made a grab, catching the whip, pulling it from the girl's belt and tossing it aside. Neither of the men nor Calamity noticed that the whip fell in plain view on the path the girl had just left.

Before Calamity could make a move in her defence, the man who held her gave a shove which crashed her into one of the piles of bales. She hit it hard, but the nature of the bales' contents prevented her from serious injury. Seeing from the very bulk of the two men that fighting was out of the question, Calamity decided to try to bluff her way out.

"Hey!" she began. "Wha—."

For a big man that whip-scarred cuss could move real fast. His right hand came around in a slap that sprawled Calamity to the ground. Stepping forward, he touched the ridge on his cheek, and drew back his left foot.

"Hold it, Jules!" the other man snapped. "Max wants to see her first."

"Yeah?" Jules snarled. "She did this to me and I'll—."

"Max'll see to it," the other interrupted, bending, gripping Calamity by the hair and hauling her to her feet. "Don't make any fuss, gal, or it'll be worse for you."

Fighting down her inclination to use her knee on the man, Calamity raised a hand to rub her cheek. Then her eyes flickered to the lane down which she came. Where in hell had Dobe and Tophet got themselves to?

Feet thudded and the other two of the quartet made their appearance from among the bales. Although Calamity did not know it, she could hardly have found herself in worse or more dangerous company. Max Gravitch ran one of the most notorious bars in New Orleans; a place the police long sought to close, but failed through lack of evidence. While dressed better, and slightly more intelligent in appearance, Gravitch could not be termed an oil-painting and there was an expression on his face that boded little good for Calamity.

"So this's St. Andre's little friend," Gravitch said, coming closer.

"This's her," Jules agreed.

"Hey!" Calamity yelped. "What's with you bunch?"

Jules shot out his hand, thrusting the girl back against the bales and bunched his big fist ready to strike. Before the tough could move, Gravitch shoved him savagely aside.

"Hold it! This might not be the one. What do you reckon, Billy?"

"Don't seem likely a gal could do it, Max," the man who had been with Jules replied. "Only we saw what she could do with a whip."

"It's her all right!" Jules snarled and waved a hand towards his face. "Reckon I wouldn't recognise the bastard who gave me this?"

"I came out worse than you," Gravitch answered, "and I couldn't be sure."

"Why was she following us just now?" asked the fourth man.

"*Me* follow *you*?" Calamity spat out. "Hell, you might go over like a house on fire with these city gals, but you're sure nowhere with me."

"Then why'd you follow us?" Gravitch inquired.

"Who's following you? I hurt myself riding that hoss and aimed to go home to rest up. Come through here looking for a cab."

"I tell you she's the one, Max!" Jules bellowed.

"Hold your voice down!" Gravitch ordered. "Whether she's the one or not, we don't want the law coming down on us."

"Look," Calamity put in. "If you'd just—."

"Shut your yap!" growled Jules, then looked at his boss. "You didn't see her using that whip, Max, or hear how it sounded."

"That's right," Gravitch agreed. "I didn't. Where's the whip at now?"

"Right here, gents," said a voice from behind them.

Never had Calamity been so pleased to hear Dobe Killem's voice, or to see her boss and Tophet Tombes, than at that moment. The words brought Gravitch and his men spinning around fast. Freighter and scout stood a few feet apart, Killem holding his coiled whip in his right hand, Tombes gripping Calamity's whip in his left and holding his right hovering above the butt of the Army Colt thrust into his waist-band in defiance of New Orleans' disapproval of people carrying firearms.

"What do you pair want?" Gravitch asked, for there were few men on the New Orleans water-front who would dare cross him.

Unfortunately for Gravitch, Killem and Tombes were only visitors and as such unaware of how they should act in the tough's presence. More than that, they came from a country which held many hard men and so grew blasé about such self-opinionated persons. In the final reckoning Killem and Tombes were, in the range sense of the word, dressed and figured themselves capable of evening the odds against them. So Killem studied the men, noted that Jules still gripped Calamity's arm in one hand, and answered Gravitch's question.

"We'll start by having that feller take his cotton-picking hand offen Calam, *hombre*," said Killem, his voice mild and gentle as that first whisper which heralds the coming of a Texas blue norther storm.

At which Calamity showed a remarkable lack of tact. Later she would apologise for her actions and explain that the rough-handling dished out by Jules prevented her from thinking straight. Maybe that was true, for the man's treatment had been far from gentle, but for once in her life Calamity spoke in a serious situation without giving due care and attention to her words.

"They're the bunch that jumped Sherry!" she yelled.

A snarl of fury left Jules' lips. "It was he——."

His angry words came to an abrupt halt. Along the river front Jules had a reputation for being rough on women and at least two street-walkers carried scars to attest his brutality; the trouble being that at long last he had picked on the wrong girl. Calamity was no street-walker living in fear of Gravitch's bunch and so meekly submitting to Jules' maulings. In her wild free life Calamity neither feared nor took abuse from any man. Only common-sense prevented her from proving that to Jules earlier.

Then Calamity stood alone against the burly quartet. Now, two good friends on hand to back her, she figured the time for meekness had ended and Jules' education could begin.

Suddenly, even as the man spoke and without giving a hint of her intentions, Calamity pivoted around. Her first move took Jules, used to more complaisant girls, by surprise. What came next prevented him from recovering his composure and making use of his extra height and strength. Coming around to face the man, although still held by the arm, Calamity drove up her right knee. While Calamity had not found time to visit a *savate* academy, she still knew how to get the best out of her shapely but powerful legs. Up lashed her knee, catching her captor right between the legs. While Jules was a tough man with a body hardened to take punishment, no amount of strength could immunise him against a blow like that. Letting out a startled and agony filled croak in place of the 'r' at the end of his interrupted final word, Jules clutched at his injured region, doubled over and staggered into the nearest bales, retching and with sweat pouring out of his agony-twisted face.

Having taken a kick in the same area during the attack on St. Andre, Gravitch found that he gathered troubles of his own. The instant Calamity felt Jules release her arm, she prepared to perform the ancient and noble feat of getting the hell out of it. Like a flash, almost before Gravitch's men, with the exception of Jules, realised fully what she had done, Calamity spun around. Dropping her shoulder, she threw herself forward and butted hard into Gravitch's injured arm. Calamity heard the man yell as she bounced away like a billiard ball heading for a cannon. Pain ripped through Gravitch as he staggered under the impact of Calamity's arrival, but his left hand shot into his jacket pocket.

"Catch!" Tombes yelled, throwing Calamity's whip handle-first to her as she came bounding in his direction. At the same moment, the scout's right hand grabbed at the butt of his Army Colt.

Even as she caught the whip, Calamity skidded into a turning halt by her two good friends. Behind the girl, Gravitch's bunch made the foolish decision to fight with guns. Billy's right hand whipped under his jacket to emerge holding a short barrelled Colt Police Pistol, .36 in calibre and the one of the few easily concealed, *working* revolvers of the period. Whether Billy had skill in its use remained a moot point, for he was not given the chance to use it.

Up and down rose Killem's whip, its lash looping forward; and in matters of that nature Killem stood second to no man.

The result proved just as effective as when Galamity handled Gravitch on the night of the attack upon St. Andre, maybe even more so for Killem's whip was heavier than the girl's, though none shorter in length. Screeching as his wrist bones splintered under the constriction of the whip, Billy felt himself hauled forward. Killem let the man come close, then ripped a punch into his belly. With an agonised croak, Billy sank to his knees, clutched at his stomach, retched violently and lost all interest in the proceedings.

Which left Gravitch and the fourth man to uphold the honour of the New Orleans underworld, Jules still being more concerned with his own troubles. For an Eastern criminal, Gravitch could lay claim to being better than fair with a gun. Only he dealt with men trained in the handling of firearms and who knew much about gun-fighting situations. Even while staggering, Gravitch sent a hand into his jacket pocket. Closing his fingers on the butt of the waiting Remington Double Derringer, Gravitch fired through the coat and by instinctive alignment. For all that, his shot came mighty close to accomplishing what several aspiring Indian brave-hearts and a couple of white bad-men tried to do. The .41 bullet missed Tophet Tombes' face by inches on its way up, ripped a hole through the brim of his hat and sent the Stetson jerking back on its storm strap.

An instant later Tombes' Army Colt gave a deep-throated answer to the Remington's challenge and the scout shot in the only way he dared under the circumstances—to kill. Tombes did not know what kind of a gun Gravitch held in the pocket, and against a man who handled one that good it did not pay to take chances. Caught between the eyes by a .44 ball, Gravitch pitched over backwards and crashed to the cotton bales at Jules' side. For a moment the gang boss hung there, then he crumpled over and fell to the ground.

The fourth member of the quartet did not even get his gun clear. Whip in hand, Calamity completed her turn. Out flicked her lash biting into the man's sleeve and sending shocking pain through him. When he brought his hand from the pocket, it came empty.

"No more!" he screeched. "I quit!"

Feet pounded and a small crowd gathered, attracted by the whip cracks and shots. A pair of policemen come forward, halting and staring at the scene before them, but they did not have time to ask questions.

"Here, boys," Calamity said. "Lay hold of 'em. Lootenant St. Andre wants to see them."

# CHAPTER FOURTEEN

*Miss Canary Meets An Intellectual Gentleman*

"NONE of the three can tell us anything," St. Andre told Calamity as he sat on the bed in her apartment and watched her dress for her role as decoy. "Max Gravitch, he was their boss, only told them they had work to do. It was a pity that Tophet had to kill Gravitch."

"He just wouldn't have it any other way," Calamity replied, drawing up her skirt and hooking one bare leg on the other, then reaching for a stocking.

"So Tophet explained. Not that I objected to Gravitch dying, our city will be a cleaner place without him. But I would rather have had him alive and talking. You see, *cherie*, it has long been my theory that there is a big man behind all the organised crime in New Orleans, a man who controls a dozen like Gravitch. One day I hope to get him."

The day would come, but not for almost two more years, when St. Andre got his man and finally solved the murder which indirectly brought him into contact with Miss Martha Jane Canary.

"No answer from Dusty yet?" Calamity inquired, drawing the stocking on and ignoring St. Andre's gaze at her legs.

"Not yet. And uncross your legs, we haven't time to think about *that*."

"This danged police work sure spoils a gal's fun," grinned Calamity.

"Then why not dr—."

"No. Sherry. We've got to get that Strangler afore he kills again and this's the only way we might do it. You didn't have no luck in tracing the last one he killed, did you?"

"None. It's the same story, the people who know won't help the police."

"Then me 'n' Jackie's going out again tonight."

Seeing from Calamity's attitude that there would be no changing her mind, St. Andre surrendered. "Very well," he said. "Go ahead. I'll tell Redon and the others not to get too far from you, and if you should meet anybody who might be the Strangler, to make sure they don't give him a chance to put that cord around your neck."

"Happen the boys are in too close, you might scare him off," Calamity pointed out.

"It's a chance we have to take, *cherie*," answered St. Andre, rising and laying a hand gently on her head. Bending over, he kissed her lightly on the lips. "I'd rather lose the Strangler than you."

"You're not getting all serious about me, now are you, Sherry?" smiled the girl, looking up at him.

"Would it be a bad thing if I did?"

"It'd be a plumb waste of both our time, and you know it. Hell, it'd never come to anything but trouble if we got too close, Sherry."

"We don't know that," St. Andre answered. "You could adapt into any society, if you wished to."

"I sure couldn't," Calamity contradicted. "And I sure as hell couldn't settle in a big city any more'n you could stop being a lawman and come West with me."

"We've—."

"We've done no more than I've done afore with men and expect to do again," the girl interrupted and gently took his hands in her own. "Mind you, Sherry, you're a long way from the worst I've known at happying up a gal. Now stop looking all solemn and go fetch my hat."

For a moment St. Andre did not move. If any other woman had spoken in the manner Calamity addressed him, he would have felt disgusted. But one did not judge Martha Jane Canary by other women's standards. Jerking her forward, he gave her a kiss, then shoved her away from him.

"Miss Canary," he stated. "You are an immoral young lady. But, Lord, there will never be another one like you."

"I'd surely be disappointed if there was," Calamity replied. "Now go get my hat while I plaster all this muck on my face. Darn it, Sherry, why do gals wear all that paint and powder?"

"To beautify themselves and attract men."

Calamity made a wry face. "Hell, I done all right without it all these years."

Before St. Andre could make any reply, a knock on the door heralded the arrival of Jackie and Redon. Both were dressed for the decoy assignment and tactfully overlooked the fact that Calamity still wore only one stocking.

"It's this boss of your's keeping me talking, Raoul," lied the unabashed Miss Canary. "You and him wait in the hall and leave a gal some privacy."

Within ten minutes a blonde Calamity, dressed as the previous night, came from her apartment with the ballet-dancing *savate* expert. Despite knowing, even more so than the previous night, the dangers facing them, the girls looked unworried and cheerful.

"Let's go," Calamity said, hooking her hand into St. Andre's arm. "Maybe we'll be lucky tonight."

Calamity proved to be a mighty poor prophetess. Although they made the rounds of the Latour Street district until past midnight, neither girl received an offer from any man resembling the Strangler's build and height. However, the night was not entirely wasted. Using her ability to make friends, Calamity started to gain the confidence of the street girls they met in the various places. While waiting for customers on one side and hoping to be selected as the Strangler's next victim in the other case, Calamity bought a few drinks, made jokes, lent a sympathetic ear to problems, and in general won over several girls. She worked for one purpose, to find out the names of possible Strangler victims.

While Calamity had never been trained for such work, she knew instinctively that she must not rush matters. One hint of suspicion would not only prevent the street-walkers taking her into their confidence, but almost might end her usefulness as a decoy. So, for the first evening, she confined herself to getting to know the other girls and persuading them that she followed their trade but did not regard them as business rivals or enemies. Buying a couple of rounds of drinks, and boasting how she had made a good sale that evening to explain where the money came from, started the thaw. From then on, once her bridge-head had been established, Calamity consolidated her position in a manner which any general would have admired. Always good company at such times, she soon had the girls laughing at her raw, unprintable jokes. In addition, she listened to the other girls' troubles, agreed that all men were lousy beasts and generally made herself agreeable. For the first time, while talking with the street-girls, Calamity learned just how rough company she had been in that afternoon. Already the story of the capture of Gravitch's gang had gone the rounds, and Calamity found that her *alter ego* stood high in the street girls' favour with only one complaint levelled at her head, that she had not treated Jules far rougher than she did. Not that the girls recognised this blonde obvious member of their profession as the famous Calamity Jane, but it made

Calamity feel good to hear their comments and receive their unconscious approbation.

However, apart from a boost to her ego, and making a lot of friends, Calamity achieved nothing that evening. No man even vaguely resembling the Strangler's height and build approached her, and shortly after midnight Redon attracted Calamity's attention with a jerk of his head.

"Well," Calamity said, shoving back her chair. "That's me for the night."

"And me," Jacqueline agreed. "If my man doesn't like it, he can do the other. What do you say, Jane?"

"Don't let *him* hear you say it," Calamity replied, winking at the others, "or the reds of your eyes'll be turning black. See you tomorrow, girls."

Calamity and Jacqueline left to the accompaniment of cheerful laughs and waves. Not until they were clear of the Latour Street district did they wait for their escort to catch up with them.

"You pair've been having fun," Redon remarked after sending one of the men to find a cab. "Did you learn anything?"

"Nothing much," Calamity admitted. "I didn't reckon rushing around asking if any of them was shy a pard or two'd get me any place. So I played it steady and maybe tomorrow I'll get me a few names."

"One of those gals, that big black-haired one, goes around with a couple of fellers we'd like to lay hands on," Redon said. "Why not—?"

"That's out!" Calamity snapped. "I'm in this thing to help you boys catch the Strangler, not go bounty hunting."

"No offence," grinned the detective, and strangely did not think any the worse of Calamity for her refusal. "Maybe we'll have a taker for you tomorrow."

"Maybe," answered Calamity. "I only hope that he hasn't got another gal tonight."

The Strangler had not struck again that evening, which did not surprise any of the decoy party. Next morning Calamity slept in late and on rising had barely finished breakfast when a messenger from St. Andre brought word that her presence was required at Headquarters. Calamity paused only long enough to collect her hat and whip before taking the cab St. Andre sent for her and driving across town. On her arrival, she found Jacqueline waiting and noticed that the slim girl wore black tights and a blouse. St. Andre sat at his desk and waved a buff-coloured telegraph message form as Calamity entered.

"This is from the Rio Hondo," he said. "It may give us the answer we need."

"Good for old Dusty," replied Calamity. "I knew he'd find the way and be only too pleased to help out."

"I have read the message and Lieutenant St. Andre showed me how the Strangler works, Calam," Jacqueline remarked. "We waited for you before trying, but I think it will work."

"Now me," grinned Calamity. "I'd be more surprised if it *didn't* work, knowing Dusty Fog like I do."

Taking the sheet of paper, Calamity read it, mouthing the words in the manner of one who spent but little time at such a pursuit. Within the limitations of using the telegraph services, Dusty Fog appeared to have done a fine job in explaining how he figured the Strangler's noose attack could be defeated. After reading the message, Calamity felt that her confidence in the Rio Hondo gun wizard had been more than justified.

"Danged if it don't look so easy you'd wonder how we missed it," she said and laid down the telegraph message form. "Let's give her a whirl, Sherry."

However, reading how to perform the counter to the attack and actually performing it, proved to be two entirely different things. Calamity's first two tries proved no more successful than her previous attempts at escaping from the constriction of the strangling cord. Much to Calamity's annoyance, Jacqueline was first to make a successful counter. With her fast dancer's reactions, she managed to perform the counter on her fifth attempt.

"It works!" she said delightedly. "I think if you did it slightly faster, Sherry, we would have a better chance."

On following the dancer's suggestion when trying the killer's hold with Calamity, St. Andre found that the counter worked much better. Previously he had been slow moving and braced for the counter. When working faster, he found less opportunity to prevent the girl escaping. The Strangler would be working fast and unprepared for resistance after so many easy kills.

"Reckon we've got the hang of it now," Calamity stated as she picked herself up from the floor after a successful counter to St. Andre's attack.

"Now that's what I call a poor choice of words," smiled the detective, also rising. "But I feel a whole lot happier now we know you've a chance of escape."

"Know something, Sherry?" said Calamity. "So do I."

That evening found Calamity and Jacqueline out on the streets again. At ten o'clock Jacqueline had a likely taker. A well dressed young man of the right height and size, slightly drunk, made the usual advances and she departed with him. Redon followed with one of the men, while Calamity spent a quarter of an hour worrying over her friend's safety. At last Jacqueline returned, unmarked and unflustered, to take a seat at Calamity's side.

"No?" asked Calamity.

"No," agreed Jacqueline. "I thought it might be when he suggested we take a walk down towards the Park. But when we got to the outside, he wanted to go to my room instead of walking. Raoul and Vic came up then, explained matters and saw him on his way."

"Could have been the Strangler playing cagey," Calamity remarked.

"They searched him thoroughly and he didn't have as much as a piece of string in his pockets. He's a clerk in a riverboat company's office and wouldn't want word of his escapade to slip out. Where now?"

"Let's try the Blue Cat, shall we?" Calamity suggested.

"Suits me," answered Jacqueline. "I wonder if we'll learn anything there?"

Half-a-dozen street girls sat around a table in the Blue Cat, a saloon much favoured by their class, when Calamity and Jacqueline entered. Apart from one, Calamity and Jacqueline had seen all the girls around the Latour Street district during their visits and five were among those Calamity befriended the previous evening. Clearly Calamity was now regarded as being all right, for cheerful greetings came her way as she and Jacqueline crossed the room.

"This's Nora, Jane," one of the girls introduced, waving a hand to the only girl Calamity and Jacqueline had not seen around the district. "She's making her debut tonight."

Looking at Nora, a small, pretty, young-looking girl wearing a blue dress and sporting a large blue ring on her right hand's third finger, Calamity smiled. "Don't know what that is, but I hope you enjoy it."

"I will," answered Nora, touching her curly blonde hair and returning Calamity's smile.

From the way she spoke, Nora clearly imagined her new life would be one of leisure and pleasure. Watching Nora, Calamity wondered if she should break her habit of letting folks run their own lives and try to steer the blonde out of a dirty, unpleasant business.

However, before Calamity could make any moves in that direction, or start to make a stab at learning the names of a few possible Strangler victims, she saw a man enter the room from Latour Street. From the way Jacqueline stiffened in her seat, Calamity guessed that the dancer also spotted the man and shared her interest. The man halted just inside the doorway and stood looking around him. Although he wore good quality clothing, the material showed signs of lack of care. His hair was long, not in the manner sported by Wild Bill Hickok and other plainsmen but merely long enough to hint at a needed visit to a barbershop. Some folk might have called him good looking, but Calamity took note of his pallid features with the intense expression and did not like what she saw. What interested Calamity and Jacqueline about the newcomer was the fact that he had a slim build and stood slightly over five foot ten in height.

Glancing at the bar to check that Redon saw the new arrival, Calamity found that after one quick look the detective turned his back on the man as if wishing to avoid recognition. The new-comer left the door and strolled in the direction of the girls' table.

"Hi, girls," he greeted.

"Hello Browne," chorused five of the table's occupants.

Calamity, a keen student of human nature and facial expressions, noticed a flicker of a scowl crease the young man's eyes as the girls used his name, however, his mouth never lost the friendly smile. He nodded in Calamity's direction.

"And who are the new faces?" he asked.

"This's Jane and Jackie," one of the girls introduced. "They've come down river from Memphis. And this is Nora, she's just starting."

"It's one way of supporting your family, Nora," the young man remarked. "The kind of money they can earn isn't enough to keep you in anything but poverty."

"You're right," Nora gasped, eyes shining in delight as she found a good excuse for turning to this kind of life instead of staying in her previous employment as a maid.

"My dear child," smiled the man, though Calamity thought it nearer a condescending sneer, "I always am."

With that he walked away, followed by several admiring, and one critical, gazes.

"Who's he?" asked Calamity.

Shock and surprise showed on most of the other girls' faces. "Why that's Browne Crossman," one gasped.

"And who's Browne Crossman?"

"Just the greatest writer who ever lived," the other girl explained. "He wrote a book, but the aristocrats won't let it be published. Works for the *Intelligencer*. Even though he's got plenty of money, he comes down here a lot. He prefers our company and he's all for the workers."

Calamity was a poker player of some skill, so she concealed her feelings. However, she had met a few of the kind of politicians who were 'all for the workers' and, being a sensible girl, mistrusted them. From her study of Browne Crossman, she decided he would be like most of his kind, self-opinionated, despising the people he professed to be all for. There had been more than a hint of condescension about him as he spoke to the girls, a touch of annoyance during the familiar use of his Christian name.

It appeared that none of the other occupants of the room had any doubts about Crossman, for he was greeted cheerfully and familiarly as he walked towards the bar. On his arrival, Crossman saw and recognised Redon, guessed the detective must be on some duty which involved keeping his identity secret, so prepared to demonstrate his love of the down-trodden underdogs.

"Well, fancy seeing you in here, Sergeant Redon," Crossman said in a voice which carried around the room. "I thought the Police Department used you in the Bourbon Street district. Or isn't that area profitable enough for you?"

Anger glinted in Redon's eyes as he turned. He knew that the young reporter deliberately identified him. "I just came in for a drink, Mr. Crossman."

"You aren't dressed as well as the last time I saw you," Crossman went on. "Isn't business as good as usual?"

A nasty snigger rose from the crowd, for all knew Crossman hinted that the detective sergeant added to his pay by taking bribes. Under other conditions Redon would have taught some of the sniggerers a sharp lesson in respect for the law, but among its other activities the *Intelligencer* liked nothing better than to expose police 'brutalities'. Such a report always meant trouble for the officer involved, so Redon held his temper, finished his drink and walked out of the room.

At her table, Calamity sat squirming angrily. Only by exercising her willpower did she prevent herself rising, crossing the room and telling Crossman what she thought of him. Redon was an honest man who never took bribes, a brave man and one doing a thankless task. In Calamity's opinion he deserved better than have to put up with the sneers of a man not fit to lick his boots.

The other girls seemed both amused and pleased to see a police-man humiliated, so Calamity kept her thoughts to herself.

Having proved himself once more 'all for the workers', Cross-man dominated the conversation in the room. He spoke well, but with only one purpose, and the customers listened attentively. With skill Crossman played on the greed and envy of his audience, condemning everybody who owned more than the people in the room, hinting that under his political party the world would be a gloriously happy place where 'the people owned everything'. To hear him talk, nobody would ever need to work if his party gained control of the country. While most of his audience drank this in eagerly, Calamity listened with a sceptical ear, wondering just what kind of world Crossman and his kind would make. Somehow she doubted if their world would be the pleasant, rosy place he painted it.

Just as Crossman started a tirade against the police as oppressors of the poor and tools of the rich, with Calamity hoping the rest of her escort would not tip their hands, screams and scuffling sounded in the street. Then the main doors flew open and a wildly excited man looked briefly in.

"Fight!" he yelled. "It's Annie Goldtooth and Louisa Duval!"

Instantly Crossman's audience came to its combined feet and headed for the door and windows at a rush. While it might be pleasant to sit listening to what a fine place the world would be when the workers got their rights, the crowd would much rather watch the exciting battle long awaited between two prominent rivals at the street girl trade.

Calamity went along with the others and saw as good a cat-fight as it had ever been her pleasure to witness from a spectator's angle. Fifteen minutes later the crowd returned to toast Annie Goldtooth's success, for she soundly defeated her rival. The first thing Calamity noticed was that Crossman had left the room. Next she glanced at where the intellectual young man had stood. A shattered glass lay on the ground; a glass which would not have broken by merely being dropped, and appeared to have been hurled furiously at the floor.

# CHAPTER FIFTEEN

*Miss Canary Meets The Strangler*

SOLEMN faces greeted Calamity as she entered the office to find St. Andre and Redon waiting. After the fight the previous night, Calamity and Jacqueline stayed on at the bar, but excitement over the sight of the battling women rode high and they found no opportunity to bring the talk around to possible victims of the Strangler. On leaving the bar, the girls and their escort found a fuming Redon waiting along the street. It took some pretty strong talk on Calamity's part to prevent the furious detective from following his intention to find and hand Crossman the thrashing of his life. After cooling Redon down, they called off the decoy and returned to Headquarters. Calamity was called in from her bed the following morning and her every instinct told her something had gone badly wrong.

"I'd like you to come to the morgue, *cherie*," St. Andre told her. "The Strangler took another victim last night."

"Another?" she gasped.

"Two youngsters found her body in the Park this morning."

"I think I saw her last night, but it's impossible to tell from the face," Redon went on. "You might be able to—."

The words died away for Redon, while admiring Calamity, did not entirely approve of a girl doing such work and also thought the sight of that body nothing to show a woman. Calamity guessed at the sergeant's thoughts and did not feel any annoyance, but she gave her agreement to St. Andre's suggestion and went with the two lawmen downstairs to the basement morgue.

Although not given to being affected by atmosphere, Calamity could hardly hold down a shudder as she entered the lamp-lit morgue. Never a cheerful spot, the basement room appeared far worse when one thought of its purpose. Calamity fought down her thoughts and walked slowly towards the sheet-draped form on the centre table. Sucking in a breath, she drew back the sheet and looked down. Blonde hair, a hideously distorted mask that seemed vaguely familiar, showed in the light. Calamity bit down an exclamation and drew the sheet from the body. A blue dress inc eased her suspicions and she found confirmation when she saw the big blue ring on the right hand. Pulling back the sheet to cover the body, Calamity turned to face the waiting detectives.

"Name's Nora. She only started on the street last night. Was working as a maid for a Colonel Yaxley's family," Calamity said. "Poor fool lil kid! I meant to try to talk her out of doing it."

"Who did she leave with?" St. Andre asked, leading Calamity from the room.

"Alone, as far as I know. She went out back and didn't come in again. The other gals laughed and made a few jokes about her losing her nerve. Lord! If that had been all she lost."

St. Andre laid a hand on Calamity's arm. "Nora?" he said. "At least we have a start. Did she say where she intended to take her customers?"

"A room in a house on Garou Street. Goldberg's place," Calamity answered.

"I know it," Redon stated. "I'll see Goldberg."

"And I'll take the Yaxleys," St. Andre went on.

A string of curses left Calamity's lips. "That poor—!" she finished.

"Easy, *cherie*," St. Andre interrupted gently.

"Easy hell!" she spat back. "Why couldn't the Strangler've picked on me last night? Maybe he will tonight."

For once in his life St. Andre looked uneasy. He did not speak until they were standing on the ground floor. Then, shrugging his shoulders, he turned to the girl and said, "*Cherie*, we must call off the decoy for the next three nights."

He did not expect Calamity to take the news calmly, and was not wrong. Anger glowed in her eyes as she swung towards him. "Why?" she asked coldly.

"General Butler is paying New Orleans a visit and I have to use every man to guard him."

Which figured when one thought how the Union Army general treated Southern prisoners-of-war and people during or after the War Between the States. While Calamity had been born in the North and supported the Union, she did not regard Butler as a hero, or even desirable, and failed to see why his life should be more important than a street walker's.

"The lieutenant's hands are tied, Calam." Redon put in. "He tried to fight against the order, but was out-ranked."

"I know he would," Calamity replied. "But we sail in three days. That means you won't have a chance to use me again."

"Some girls would be pleased of that," St. Andre told her gently. "At least we now have the name of a victim. It might lead us to the killer."

133

"Yeah," answered Calamity. "It might at that."

If St. Andre had not been so busy following up the lead in the Strangler case, than helping organise the protection of the visiting general, he might have thought about Calamity's meek acceptance and decided that it was not in keeping with her character as he knew it.

On leaving Headquarters, Calamity took a cab to the river front and joined Killem's men. She said nothing about the decoy work being cancelled and, although she and Killem went to watch the arrival of General Butler, they did not have a chance to speak with any of their detective friends. However, Calamity saw why the Chief of Police insisted on maximum security. A large crowd of hostile demonstrating sufferers at Butler's hands during and just after the War swarmed on the river front, and it took a good force of club-swinging policemen to hold them back as the hated figure left the riverboat. (A noticeable side-issue was that the *Intelligencer*, usually so rabid in exposing police 'brutalities,' never said a word about the clubs cracking heads in defence of General Butler). The defence and protection of Butler had been left in the hands of the municipal authorities because various wise heads realised that the sight of Butler taken with Union Army uniforms might provoke serious trouble.

Having grown used to Calamity dressing and leaving on the decoy work, none of her freighter friends saw anything unusual in it that evening. Calamity debated whether she should take a gun or not, but decided against it. So she set forth into the night, walking through the Park and entering the Blue Cat to find only a handful of girls and a few riverboat men present.

"The Street's quiet tonight," she remarked, taking a seat with the other girls and ordering a beer from a bored waiter.

"There's a big crowd gone up to the Opera House to show that bastard Butler what folks down here think of him," one of the other girls answered.

After sipping at her beer, Calamity pretended to notice something. "Hey, has Nora got a taker already?"

None of the girl's answered for a moment, then a buxom blonde called Hetty said, "She's not been home all night, or today. I room next to her."

"Maybe the Strangler got her," another put in. "That Redon was around asking about her this morning. They came round just after Betty Muldoon disappeared."

"And when Sarah Gotz stopped coming here," a third girl

remarked thoughtfully. "I knew Sarah hadn't just run out like her man told the law."

Once the subject had been opened, the girls started to discuss it thoroughly and in doing so told Calamity all she need to know. Sitting quietly, she made a mental note of the various names mentioned. Not all would be Strangler victims but she reckoned she had learned enough to start St. Andre on the trail.

"I'm getting scared to go with a feller," Hetty stated. "Why in hell don't the police stop him?"

Only just in time did Calamity prevent herself answering that the police might have brought the Strangler's career to an end earlier if given assistance by various members of the public. She read the fear in each girl's face and realised it came through the detectives asking about a Strangler victim by name. Before the girls did not know if a friend be dead or merely missing, now they knew for sure. Calamity decided to get word to St. Andre as soon as possible to strike while the iron of fear burned hot, as he would find the girls more co-operative now.

All eyes jerked around as the main doors opened and Calamity detected almost a gasp of relief as the lank figure of Browne Crossman entered. The young man looked even more than usually sullen and moody as he crossed the room, but managed to greet the girls in a friendly manner. Taking a seat with them, he accepted Hetty's offer of a beer and joined in the discussion of the identity of the killer. Crossman expressed the view that the killer might be a religious bigot trying to improve the world by removing its undesirable fallen women. From the way Crossman spoke, Calamity decided that he did not approve of religion and was suspicious of anybody who followed Christian beliefs.

Then one of the girls, perhaps bored by Crossman's bombastic domination of the conversation, dropped in a remark about Butler's visit. With the exception of Calamity, every girl at the table had been born and raised in the South, so their views on Butler varied only by the speaker's power of invective. Watching Crossman, Calamity saw the anger in his eyes and in the way he gripped his glass between his fingers.

"Why doesn't your paper do something about Butler, Browne?" Hetty asked. "If it hadn't been for him letting his men loot my father's store, I'd never've had to go on the streets."

Normally such a story would have brought much sympathy from Crossman, but in other cases the girl's persecutor had been someone whose political or social views did not coincide with the young man's.

"I'll ask the editor about it," he answered.

At that moment the doors opened and a number of men entered. One of the men, sporting a bruised lump on his forehead gathered when trying to rush Butler through the police cordon, invited the girls to take a drink with him. At the bar, Calamity listened to the profane flow of ideas about Butler's morals, parentage, destination after death and general habits. Suddenly she realised that Crossman had not come to the bar and was not in sight. This surprised her, for Crossman had not been slow to accept free drinks from the girls and she expected him to take his chance when the newcomer offered to pay.

Deciding she would see where the reporter went, Calamity remarked, "Reckon I'll take a stroll and raise the rent."

Before any of the men at the bar could make her an offer, Calamity crossed to the door and passed out on the Latour Street. For a moment she stood at the door, undecided which way to go. Seeing no sign of Crossman, she turned and made for another gathering place for street girls.

Just as she passed a side alley, she saw a dark shape and heard Crossman's voice. "Hi there, Jane. Looking for trade?" he said.

"A gal has to pay for her room somehow," Calamity replied.

"If you come to my room, I'll see you don't have that problem."

"That's me you hear knocking on the door," Calamity said. "Let's go."

"Come this way," Crossman ordered. "I don't mind, but there are folks in town who would use my going with you against me."

"I reckon there are," agreed Calamity and walked into the alley.

Clearly Crossman knew his way around the back alleys behind Latour Street, for he did not falter as he led Calamity through the area. Although there was still a full moon, Crossman kept to the shadows and slowed his pace whenever he saw anybody ahead of him. In this manner he led Calamity down to the road which separated Latour Street from the City Park. Halting in the darkness of an alley, Crossman looked both directions along the street before turning to Calamity.

"My place's across the Park," he said. "Let's walk through to it, shall we?"

Acting her part, Calamity hesitated. "Well—I—."

"Scared of the Strangler?" asked Crossman mockingly. "Maybe I'm him."

"Aw! Don't say things like that, Browne," gasped Calamity. "You couldn't be the Strangler."

"Then let's go, or I'll go alone."

"Don't get mad. I'm coming."

More than three years of living with danger as a companion had given Calamity an instinct for trouble. She noticed the way Crossman hustled her across the street at a time when nobody either stood or walked nearby and it occurred to her that at no time had any person seen her with the young man. Uneasy stirrings gave Calamity a warning and she remembered that Crossman fitted the size which Tophet Tombes claimed for the Strangler. All too well Calamity knew Tombes' skill as a reader of sign, he would not make a mistake about so basic and important a matter as estimating the height and weight of the man he tracked.

Yet could this slim man, who preached such stupid ideas as making life easier for owlhoots and not hanging murderers, be the fiend who slaughtered nine girls in the Park?

Down on Latour Street, just as Calamity and Crossman entered the Park, men began chanting, "We'll hang that bastard Butler on a sour-apple tree."

Calamity felt Crossman's hand tighten on her arm and heard the sudden hiss of his breath.

"They sure don't like old Butler, do they," she said.

"The scum!" Crossman hissed back. "The lousy scum. Don't they realise that General Butler is a great man?"

"Maybe they remember how he treated them while he was down here in the War," Calamity answered. "He gave 'em cause to hate him."

After an unsuccessful career as a combat soldier, General Butler had been appointed Governor of New Orleans under the Union Army of Occupation. Amongst other acts, Butler siezed some eight hundred thousand dollars which had been deposited in the Dutch Consul's office, the money going into his personal bank account. His final act, which brought his recall to Washington, was an order stating 'If any woman give insult or offence to an officer or soldier of the Union Army, she shall be regarded and be held liable to be treated as a woman of the streets playing her avocation.' Crossman knew all that, regarding the theft of the money, and later stories of corruption, as lies spawned by Butler's enemies, and regarding Butler, currently a Radical Republican, as a great, noble and misunderstood man whose views almost coincided with Crossman's own.

Believing anybody he regarded highly must be perfect, Crossman's anger rose at the insults piled on General Butler since his arrival in New Orleans for a visit.

Taking his hand from Calamity's arm, Crossman allowed the

girl to move slightly ahead of him. He dipped his hand into his jacket and pulled out the length of stout, knotted whip cord which served him so well on other occasions when a member of the working class scum needed punishing. How he hated those stupid fools he came into contact with on Latour Street. Not one of them cared that he and his kind intended to make the world a better place for them. All they thought about was their pleasure. Take last night. Instead of listening to him and being prepared to follow his lead, those scum ran into the street to see two women fighting. Well, one of them paid the price for that insult. When Crossman and his party came into power, in addition to making the world a better place for the workers, he would see that those bunch from the Blue Cat paid for their indifference; just as this slut was going to pay right now.

Out flickered the cord, its deadly noose circling then dropping around the brim of Calamity's hat and down to her shoulders. Swiftly Crossman gathered the two ends of the cord, swinging so his back faced Calamity's and carrying the cord up on to his shoulder as he had done nine times before. Soon he would feel the cord tighten and the girl's frantic, but unavailing, struggles which would become weaker until she hung limp and dead.

"You're like all the rest!" he snarled as the noose flickered out and dropped into place.

Although Calamity partially suspected Crossman, and had practised escaping from the Strangler's attack until she felt it would be almost second nature to do so, the feel of the cord dropping around her gave her a nasty shock. It was like the first time she became involved in an Indian attack on the freight outfit. Sure she had known what to do in such conditions, but the actual happening handed her a hell of a jolt.

For all that Calamity did not freeze or panic. Instead she went into action fast, using the technique suggested in his message by Dusty Fog. Giving a fervent prayer that Dusty, as he mostly did, knew what he talked about when he sent off the instructions, Calamity made her move.

Thrusting herself back, instead of pulling away—as the other victims had instinctively done, thereby tightening the noose and speeding their end—Calamity rose on her toes and thrust her shoulders back against Crossman's. At the same moment her hands shot up, back over her shoulders, closed on and gripped the cords between her neck and Crossman's hands. Before he could lean forward and gain the extra leverage which made the use of the *thuggi* cord so deadly effective, Crossman received a shock. Swiftly

Calamity tightened her hold on the cord, then jerked both feet from the ground, bending her knees, and letting her dead weight hang on Crossman's back. Taken by surprise by Calamity's weight and the unexpected move, Crossman could not prevent himself being dragged over backwards. He lost his grip on the cord as he and the girl both went rump-first to the ground.

Following the plan she made while walking through the Park on her way to the Blue Cat earlier that evening, Calamity released one end of the cord and jerked it from around her neck. Hat and blonde wig went flying as she removed the cord, but Calamity did not care how she looked at that moment, being more concerned in summoning assistance.

"Help!" she yelled, and Calamity had quite a voice when needed. "The Strangler's here!"

Letting out a snarl, Crossman rolled on his side and rose. He swung to face the girl and stared at the sight before him. Gone were the hat and wig, and even through the paint and powder on Calamity's face Crossman recognised her. Fury ripped into him as he faced the girl he had seen with St. Andre on the night some fancied insult led him to take his eighth victim. It appeared that the stupid, inefficient, bungling police had out-witted him, laid a trap into which he fell.

Then shock bit into Crossman as he realised just how close to the edge of the Park he made his murder attempt. On every previous occasion the distance would not have mattered, for his victim struggled but died in silence. Success on nine occasions had made him lax, anger caused him to be unthinking.

Footsteps thudded on the path and Crossman looked by Calamity to where half-a-dozen brawny men raced in his direction. For a moment Crossman hesitated, then panic hit him and he started to turn to run. Maybe if Crossman had stood his ground he would have been able to talk his way out, but he lacked the kind of nerve to take such a chance.

Even as Crossman turned to run, Calamity sprang forward and grabbed him by his jacket's lapels. Desperation and terror flooded over Crossman as he heard the angry yells of the approaching men. Grabbing Calamity's wrists, he tried to drag her hands from him, but failed. Mouthing terrified curses, he lashed out wildly with a foot and caught the girl full on the shin-bone. Calamity screamed as the agony bit into her. Pain caused her to lose her hold and Crossman thrust her aside, whirled and prepared to flee for his life. He left it too late, the six men swarmed by the staggering Calamity and at him.

"She's ly—!" Crossman began.

But the men had seen the cord, read its message and knew the truth. Out shot a big fist, smashing full into Crossman's mouth and shattering his words half said. Crossman reeled backwards, more blows landed on him. No man could think of the nine dead victims of the Strangler without feeling an uncontrollable hatred for the one who killed them. Not even being 'all for the workers' could save Crossman from the fury of the men. He went down screaming, then a boot smashed into him and another came driving out to strike his temple with shattering force.

"No!" Calamity screamed, trying to walk on her kick-damaged leg.

Turning, one of the men came back and gently caught her by the arms. "Easy gal," he said. "The bastard won't harm you now."

A policeman came racing up, blowing on his whistle as he ran. Skidding to a halt, he looked first at Calamity, then to where the men stood around the still shape on the ground.

"Just stay right where you are, boys," he said, walking forward to kneel by Crossman's side and examine the unmoving form.

"That's the Strangler," one of the men said. "We stopped him killing the girl there."

"I sure hope you're right about that," answered the policeman. "He's dead."

# CHAPTER SIXTEEN

## *Miss Canary's Departure*

ST. ANDRE sat by Calamity as she lay back on the bed in her appartment. It was the evening after Crossman's death and St. Andre came to visit the girl to give her the latest details of the affair. He found Calamity wearing her usual style of dress and nursing her injured shin, but otherwise none the worse for her experience.

"We searched Crossman's apartment last night," he told Calamity. "Among other things we found his diary, quite a document I can tell you. In fact it gives us complete proof that he was the Strangler."

"Does it tell you why he did it?"

"Patience, *cherie*," grinned the detective, then became sober again. "From what he wrote, Crossman believed himself to be ordained to make the world a much better place for the rest of we weak mortals to live in. He intended to change everything, improve the lot of the poor folks. Only he found that they didn't exactly fall over themselves with eagerness to let him improve their lot."

"Figured all along he didn't care for the folks down at the Blue Cat, no matter how he acted," Calamity remarked.

"You figured right. One night while he was there, he slipped and spilled a drink over him, and the customers laughed. They had the audacity to laugh at the great Browne Crossman, and I quote from his diary. He had been reading about the *thuggi* and made up a cord, this was before he went to the Blue Cat that night. The cord was in his pocket. Apparently he had been seeing a girl in secret and while they walked in the Park, she started teasing him about his accident. In a rage, he killed her. After that, she being his first victim, every time anything went wrong for him, or he detected insolence in the attitude of the 'workers', he picked up another girl and killed her."

"Why'd he pick on the gals, Sherry?"

"That he doesn't explain, but I believe he found it safer, less dangerous than trying it with men. He says that the girls never suspected him and went willingly into the Park with him."

"How'd you reckon he got that way?" asked Calamity.

"I don't know," St. Andre answered. "I've seen several of those young intellectuals in college and since. They're all the same, hating anybody who possessed more than they, despising the poor and under-privileged they pretend to wish to help. Crossman was that kind. When he found that people didn't regard him as their saviour he grew to hate them and took that way of getting revenge."

"What'll happen about the men who killed him?"

"That depends on the trial, *cherie*. But I can't see any jury convicting them for killing the Strangler. And now, what would you like to do tonight?"

"Aren't you guarding Butler?"

"He was recalled upriver this afternoon, and I have taken some much deserved vacation time. From now until you leave, I am at your service. Shall we go to the opera, or try gambling at one of the clubs on Bourbon Street?"

Calamity smiled. "Let's sit and call each other liars instead."

Standing on the river front, St. Andre watched the powerful paddleboat take up the strain and drew the trio of horse-loaded flat-boats from the quay. Suddenly a whip cracked by his ear and he looked to where Calamity stood at the stern of the last boat. The girl had been busy helping the horses and unable to speak to him before. Now she stood with one foot on the rail, the whip which saved St. Andre from a brutal beating held in her hand.

"Horray wah, Sherry!" she yelled.

"*Au revoir, cherie!*" he called back.

Not until the boats disappeared in the distance did St. Andre turn. His head throbbed from the previous night's celebration party at the Cheval D'Or. While he boasted being able to take his liquor, he had to admit those Western freighters made him look like a beginner. The party lasted late and Jacqueline danced herself into exhaustion. She had cause to celebrate. The New Orleans authorities offered a thousand dollars reward for the apprehension of the Strangler and with typical generosity Calamity insisted on giving the dancer half. At last Jacqueline had enough money to take formal ballet lessons and St. Andre arranged for her to meet with the head of the visiting ballet group.

After the excitement and happiness came the sorrow of parting. Calamity had gone and he doubted if they would ever meet again.

"Philippe darling!" a voice said turning St. Andre found a

beautiful young woman at his side. "I looked for you at the ballet last night, you naughty boy. Now I insist you buy me lunch to make up for my disappointment."

At one time St. Andre would have been very pleased to escort the girl anywhere. Now he regarded her with cold eyes. How pallid and insipid she seemed after knowing Calamity Jane. Then the detective shrugged. Calamity had gone from his life for ever. He might just as well take what was left, for there would never be another girl like Calamity.

# A SELECTION OF FINE READING
# AVAILABLE IN CORGI BOOKS

## War

| | | | |
|---|---|---|---|
| ☐ 552 07943 X | BATTLE | C. S. Forester, Robert Carse etc. | 5/- |
| ☐ 552 07871 9 | COMRADES OF WAR | Sven Hassel | 5/- |
| ☐ 552 07935 9 | MERCENARY (illustrated) | Mike Hoare | 7/6 |
| ☐ 552 07959 6 | THREE CAME HOME | Agnes Keith | 5/- |
| ☐ 552 07986 3 | HIROSHIMA REEF | Eric Lambert | 5/- |
| ☐ 552 07726 7 | THE DIRTY DOZEN | E. M. Nathanson | 7/6 |
| ☐ 553 07910 3 | THE GERMAN ARMY AND THE NAZI PARTY | | |
| | | (illustrated) Robert J. O'Neill | 7/6 |
| ☐ 552 07967 7 | NIGHT FIGHTER | C. F. Rawnsley and Robert Wright | 5/- |
| ☐ 552 07476 4 | THE SCOURGE OF THE SWASTIKA (illustrated) | | |
| | | Lord Russell of Liverpool | 5/- |
| ☐ 552 07477 2 | THE KNIGHTS OF BUSHIDO (illustrated) | Lord Russell | 5/- |

## Westerns

| | | | |
|---|---|---|---|
| ☐ 552 07977 4 | SMILING DESPERADO | Max Brand | 3/6 |
| ☐ 552 07756 9 | SUDDEN—TROUBLESHOOTER | Frederick H. Christian | 3/6 |
| ☐ 552 07976 6 | SUDDEN AT BAY | Frederick H. Christian | 3/6 |
| ☐ 552 07991 X | THE HOODED RIDERS | J. T. Edson | 3/6 |
| ☐ 552 08011 X | THE BULL WHIP BREED | J. T. Edson | 3/6 |
| ☐ 552 08012 8 | SAGEBRUSH SLEUTH | J. T. Edson | 3/6 |
| ☐ 552 07856 5 | MAN OF THE FOREST | Zane Grey | 3/6 |
| ☐ 552 07653 8 | MACKENNA'S GOLD | Will Henry | 3/6 |
| ☐ 552 07902 2 | SHALAKO | Louis L'Amour | 3/6 |

## Crime

| | | | |
|---|---|---|---|
| ☐ 552 07872 7 | THE KREMLIN LETTER | Noel Behn | 5/- |
| ☐ 552 07974 X | PHOTO FINISH | Jean Bruce | 3/6 |
| ☐ 552 07855 7 | STRIP TEASE | Jean Bruce | 3/6 |
| ☐ 552 07990 1 | A CASE FOR THE BARON | John Creasey | 3/6 |
| ☐ 552 07960 X | MURDER TOO LATE | John Creasey | 3/6 |
| ☐ 552 07912 X | WIDOWS WEAR WEEDS A. A. Fair (Erle Stanley Gardner) | | 3/6 |
| ☐ 552 07716 X | AMBER NINE | John Gardner | 3/6 |
| ☐ 552 07224 9 | THE LIQUIDATOR | John Gardner | 3/6 |
| ☐ 552 07905 7 | HIDEAWAY | John Gardner | 3/6 |
| ☐ 552 07988 X | UNDERCOVER CAT PROWLS AGAIN | The Gordons | 3/6 |
| ☐ 552 07677 5 | DIE RICH, DIE HAPPY | James Munro | 3/6 |
| ☐ 552 07945 6 | THE DRUMS OF FU MANCHU | Sax Rohmer | 3/6 |
| ☐ 552 07911 1 | IT WON'T GET YOU ANYWHERE | Desmond Skirrow | 5/- |
| ☐ 552 07973 1 | THE BODY LOVERS | Mickey Spillane | 4/- |
| ☐ 552 07753 4 | THE TWISTED THING | Mickey Spillane | 3/6 |
| ☐ 552 07831 X | THE BY-PASS CONTROL | Mickey Spillane | 3/6 |

*All these books are available at your bookshop or newsagent; or can be ordered direct from the publisher. Just tick the titles you want and fill in the form below.*

••••••••••••••••••••••••••••••••••••••••••••••••••••••••••••••••••••••••••••••••••••

CORGI BOOKS, Cash Sales Department, J. Barnicoat (Falmouth) Ltd., P.O. Box 11, Falmouth, Cornwall.

Please send cheque or postal order. No currency, and allow 6d. per book to cover the cost of postage and packing in U.K., 9d. per copy overseas.

NAME ...................................................................................................................

ADDRESS ...........................................................................................................

(SEPT. 68) ...........................................................................................................